THE *Dirty Heroes* COLLECTION

SKELETON
KING

CHARITY B.

The Dirty Heroes
COLLECTION

Once upon a time, a scorned Queen opened a box, unleashing horrible evil on the world's heroes.

Instead of gallantry and chivalry, they now possessed much more perverse traits. They've fallen victim to their darkest and most deviant desires.

This is one of their stories...

BLURB

Skeleton King

In this town, I'm free from shame
A place where everyone knows my name

Glamorizing corpses to feed a need
That's why they call me Skeleton King

They all worship me, but they don't know the real me
All they see is my painted face

Truth is, I'm terrified, all the hope inside me died
Death and cold will forever be my morbid fate
Then she showed me something more
Somehow stealing death's allure

Trigger Warning: This book contains many triggers and this warning should be taken seriously. The sexual and graphically depicted scenes in this novel are not for the squeamish and will be disturbing for some readers.

AUTHOR'S
note

I cannot express how excited I was when I found out I was going to have the opportunity to write a story inspired by some of my ALL-TIME favorite characters. This was a blast for me, and I hope you have as much fun reading this as I had writing it. While you don't need to watch *The Nightmare Before Christmas* to enjoy this book, seeing the film first will make the experience that much better.

Trigger Warning
This book contains many triggers, and this warning should be taken seriously. The sexual and graphically depicted scenes in this novel are not for the squeamish and will be disturbing for some readers.

Dedication

This one goes out to Murphy Wallace and all of the other incredible authors involved in The Dirty Heroes Collection. This was such a dream come true to write. Skeleton King is inspired by one of my all-time favorite films, and it would likely not have ever been written if not for this collection. Thank you for including me in this amazing project.

"Oh, somewhere deep inside these bones,
an emptiness began to grow."

Jack Skellington

GRAVE ROBBER

John Skelver

October 31st, 1993 ~ Morning

COOL FALL WIND BLOWS AGAINST MY perspiring skin, sending a chill up my spine. My face paint is most likely smeared from the heavy sweat dripping down my cheeks. As the early-morning fog floats around the tombstones, my shovel digs deeper into the earth.

She lies beneath my feet, waiting for me. Her death was untimely, so said her obituary. A young woman full of life and a promising future, until some teenage kid decided he wasn't too drunk to drive. She was killed instantly.

It was definitely disappointing that her

family chose a closed casket, presumably because there was significant damage to her face. The funeral was as beautiful as the photo they displayed of her, though. Wavy brown hair accentuated her chocolate eyes and mocha skin that looked delicious enough to eat.

Her name was Natasha.

I'm grateful, however, that they buried her so quickly after her death. There's a very small window of time I have to work with before things get excessively messy.

I sigh in relief when the steel of the shovel *thuds* against the hard oak of her coffin. "Thank God," I murmur. Grunting, I lift myself out of the hole that I've spent the last six hours digging. As the orange sun begins to peek over the horizon, the sky lightens to a bluish gray, telling me my time is nearly up.

Nothing, my albino bull terrier, stands at attention, his ears up and alert. He'll let me know if anyone is coming.

My crow bar *clinks* against the zipper of my bag before I jump back into the grave. Using it to pry open the box in which Sasha sleeps, I shudder at the casket *creaking* loud in the dead silence of the dawn. The moment I lift the heavy lid, my heart tumbles around in my chest.

"Hi, Natasha."

She's perfect. Still so fresh and new. I wonder who she was when she could still inhale oxygen? Was she outgoing or shy? Smart or dense? From the ornery smile in her photo and how she was spoken of during her eulogy, I've deduced that she was polite and classy in her everyday life, but those she was closest to knew she also had a wild side. She liked to have fun.

"It's time to go."

Groaning, I lift her high enough above my head to place her on the edge of her grave, my arms straining in protest when I pull myself from the pit in the earth.

Nothing sniffs Natasha's body as I kneel next to her. Her white dress is stark, sprawled across the dark dirt. I steal a moment to take her in, trailing my hand lightly over her body. The strands of her hair are soft beneath my fingers while the flesh of her cheeks has lost all suppleness. I can barely make myself wait until she's in my bed to take her.

It's been awhile since I've had a woman. My

work keeps me busy. I've created quite a name for myself in my little town of Hallows Grove.

"God, you're so beautiful."

Right on schedule, memories of my mother's voice echo in my mind. *I can't even look at you! You repulse me.* I wonder if I'll ever be free of her disgrace.

Grave picking for passion as opposed to business has its own set of risks. When it's personal, the need is more about attraction. Attraction to who they could have been while still alive. That causes me to take certain risks that I would avoid if it were a paying job.

When I first started doing this, I would attempt to close the graves once I retrieved the body, but not only was it much too time consuming, with the loose dirt, it was still obvious the plot had been tampered with, so now I just leave them open.

Straightening the tarp, I drag her corpse to the center before wrapping her inside. Heaving her over my shoulder, I follow the lanterns I've arranged to light my way and safely secure her in the trunk of my black Buick Grand National.

Once all my tools are returned to my duffle

bag, I whistle at Nothing. "Come on, boy. Let's go home." He hops in the seat next to me, tail wagging as I reach across the car to crank down his window and turn on the radio. The end of a song fades out as the deejay comes on. Pulling onto the dirt road that leads from the cemetery, I light a joint before rolling down my own window.

Happy Halloween to all you early risers out there! I hate to start the day off with such a tragedy, but we just received some heartbreaking news here at NBXS. River Phoenix was pronounced dead at one fifty-one this morning. The twenty-three-year-old actor is said to have overdosed outside the Viper Room in Hollywood. We'll have more on the story later. First, the new hit single from Salt-N-Pepa's brand new album. Here's Whatta Man!

Nope. I turn off the radio to dig in my console for The Police cassette, careful to blow the pot smoke away from Nothing.

The crazy dog hangs his head out the window the entire drive. The closer I get to the private community I call home, the harder my cock grows. I'll sleep with Natasha once or twice before the work begins. It's a time-consuming process to taxidermize humans, and once I start, I won't be able to fuck her again until I've finished.

A wall of trees hides our town from the eyes of Mundaners, those who don't take up residence in Hallows Grove. There are two gated points of entry set at the north and south ends. The south entrance is located behind The Row, the only part of town outside the gates. It's where all our government buildings such as the new town hall, the post office, police station and so on are located.

Pulling up to the code box at the south entrance, I enter my password. The large, twisted gate opens, *creaking* as jack-o'-lanterns impaled by iron spikes sit along the top.

Ghost-shaped lights are strung from the streetlamps with random, Styrofoam headstones dotting the side of the road. Skeletons—some plastic, some not—swing from the branches of the large tree growing in the middle of town. The transformation of Hallows Grove during this season feels like the only time that our town truly reflects what it holds on the inside.

Ghoulish decorations overtake every home.

Giant spiders crawl across roofs, ghosts swing from porches, and there are *so many* jack-o'-lanterns. Monster mannequins stand on front lawns with mechanical witches stirring their brews as I turn onto Nightshade Circle.

Halloween is the one holiday we don't take lightly. It's been nearly twelve years since I've lived elsewhere, and I often forget how different things are here. My desires are seen as perversions in the Mundane World. I would be a pariah if I ever tried to survive out there.

But here? I'm a king.

After parking in my driveway, I walk to the back of the car with Nothing jumping out right behind me. As I unlock the trunk, a soft *pew* sounds at the exact moment a sharp sting snaps the nape of my neck. Hissing in pain, I press my hand against the throbbing in an attempt to relieve it.

"What the fuck?!"

Cackling laughter fills the air as preteen triplets, Bolt, Jolt, and Cask, run into my cemetery replicated yard wearing mischievous grins.

"Gotcha!" Jolt laughs, skipping toward me

with a BB gun in her hand.

Bolt is right behind her, opening and closing his pocket knife. "Did ya?"

"Get a new?" Cask asks, licking a lollipop as he walks over to my partially open trunk.

Jolt bats her eyelashes as if she didn't just shoot me. "Body, Skeleton King?"

I roll my eyes, but my pride makes me smile. "She's in the car. Do you want to see?"

All three of them jump up in excitement, asking their question one piece at a time.

"Is this one?"

"Going to be?"

"Your girlfriend?"

Lifting the trunk fully open, I smile, moving the tarp to reveal her. "Yes, for as long as she lasts."

Cask slurps his candy as he reaches down to lift Natasha's dress, and I smack his hand. "Don't even fucking think about it."

"Can we?" Cask pouts while attempting to take away Bolt's knife.

Jolt gives me an evil grin, twirling her purple dress. "At least watch?"

"You do her?" Bolt asks as he shoves his

brother to the ground.

I've gotten used to the way of life here. There isn't anything too perverse, too macabre for Hallows Grove.

"Absolutely not," I declare as Bolt follows me up my front steps, stabbing his knife into the trim of the door while Jolt points her gun at the back of Cask's head, imitating shooting sounds. "Shouldn't you guys be home helping your Dad get ready for tonight's games?" I turn to Bolt who is still assaulting my house. "Stop that, you little shit."

He sticks the blade in one more time with a defiant grin. "Dad wants us to make sure."

"You'll be there early," Jolt adds, climbing onto my porch.

Cask pops his head between his siblings, still licking that stupid lollipop. "To take pictures."

I open my front door to step inside, quickly cracking it closed enough that they don't take it as an invitation to follow me. They're known around town as the 'Sanity Eaters' for a reason.

"I know the drill. I'll be there. Now, get out of here."

Slamming the door behind me, I grab the

stretcher from the corner of my parlor. I have about ten hours until I need to be at Ogier Bognar's house for the Halloween Games.

As I push the cot outside, I hear the Bognar triplets yelling as they make their way across my neighbors' front yards. My eyes land on Sarah Stein standing in the street, looking her beautifully awkward self as she shuffles toward Fink's house.

While I've always found living women attractive, they're terrifying beings. They'll cut you deeper than any blade ever could and laugh while you bleed. I've been tortured my entire life by the monstrous creatures. Sarah, though, she's always been kind. I've never seen her be cruel or vicious. In some ways, that makes her more frightening, even if intriguing.

Her bright red hair frames her face while I hold my hand up in greeting. Lifting her head, she smiles at me before picking up her pace. She must have gotten out again. Fink isn't keen on giving her much freedom, even in town. I don't agree with how he treats her, I never have, but I have my own vices, leaving me with no room for judgement.

Reaching into my trunk, I caress Natasha's face. If she could think or feel I wonder if she would be jealous of my thoughts traveling to another woman.

"We're home."

I slide my arms beneath her body, lifting her onto the gurney and wheeling her inside to the bathroom. She'll be brought to my office tomorrow morning so I can begin my work on her, today, however, she'll spend with me.

Nothing's nails *tap* on the hardwood floor in the hall as I take off Natasha's dress. Damn, her tits are amazing. I won't touch her right now, though. The anticipation always makes it better.

I'm aware she can't feel the warmth of the water, yet I still make it a comfortable temperature before I soap off her skin. Lightly pulling on her eyelashes, I lift her eyelid to remove the spikey cap that's keeping it closed. The warm brown color her irises once were are now dulled with a cloudy overlay. Regardless, I prefer them open. Her hair and makeup still look nice, so for the time being, I leave the rest of her head alone.

"Do you want to hear a secret?" I ask, rinsing

the suds from her blue tinted flesh, revealing the livor mortis. "I wish I could make you come alive so I don't have to pretend to have intimacy anymore."

That's something I would never admit aloud to anyone that could repeat it. My being with women whose souls have left this earth is not only a large part of who I am, but it's also my only source of affection.

Once the bath is drained, I lift her onto the cot, drying her off before wheeling the gurney to my room. Closing my door behind us, I gently lay her on my clean sheets. I don't understand why I get nervous each time. She won't be able to humiliate or deny me, and still, I wonder if she would have found me worthy while she was walking this earth.

Every time you rape yourself, you blacken your soul.

I rarely think of my mother's persecution outside of sexual situations. It's fucked up, and I have no idea how to stop it.

As I take off my clothes, shame prickles along my nerves. I remind myself for the millionth time that this is a victimless crime.

Natasha, who she was before death carried her away, will have no knowledge of me. Her family won't either.

Settling above her body, I kiss her sealed lips for a few moments before I wrap her fingers around my straining cock. In some ways, Natasha is like a toy. I move her and touch her however I want without worry of complaint. She has no needs, no desires, and that's what makes her perfect. I press my lips to her neck, kissing my way down her chest to suck a nipple in between my lips.

"Do you like that?"

Leaning back on my knees, I lift each of her legs to spread them apart which reveals a trimmed patch of dark hair framing her grayish pussy. I softly hold her hip as I line myself up with her entrance. Her flesh is cold, and the moment I push into her corpse, it feels like dough molding around my erection.

"God, you feel so fucking good."

Her limp body rocks beneath me on each thrust, her breasts wobbling up and down as her milky eyes stare at the ceiling. Lifting one of her legs, I hold it around my waist, allowing me to shove in deeper.

My own son? How did I raise such perverse filth?

It's been awhile since I've had sex, so it doesn't take long before the feeling of her encasing me has me pouring my warm come into her chilled pussy. I don't know why my orgasms always force my thoughts toward my mother, yet every time, I can't stop the memories from flooding through my mind.

"But pleeeaaassse, Mom? Come on! It's Halloween!" It isn't fair. I'm seven now, why do I still have to go to bed so early?

"Don't you dare raise your voice to me. You have to be up for school in the morning. Now take off your costume, and go brush your teeth. I'll be there in a minute to read the scriptures."

I want to stomp my feet and slam my door, but I know I'll get a whipping. I drop my pillowcase with a thud on the floor. I huff, looking at all the candy that I have to wait until tomorrow to eat. Peeling off my cowboy costume, I drop my pretend revolver on the dresser and pick out my blue and yellow striped pajamas.

Once I wash my face and brush my teeth, I obey my mom, waiting for her in my room.

"You're drinking again? Are you serious?!" her voice screeches beneath the door. "I've told you, I will not tolerate devil water in this house!"

"How the fuck else am I supposed to get through this shit show of a life, Aziza?" my dad bellows before something crashes like it's breaking. "This is all on you, bitch."

I cover my ears so I can't hear the mean things they say to each other. I hate that they do this so much. At least it isn't too much longer before my door opens, and my mother comes in with the Bible.

She looks okay. If I hadn't just heard them, I would never have known they were fighting. "Are you all right, Mom?"

Sitting in the chair next to my bed, she smooths out her skirt. "You don't need to concern yourself, Johnathan." She flips the book open to a marked page, reading one of the highlighted passages. "Put to death, therefore, whatever belongs to your earthly nature: sexual immorality, impurity, lust, evil desires and greed, which is idolatry. Colossians 3:5."

I don't really understand the words in the Bible half the time, but I won't ever ask. It's always about evil and sins. For once, I just wish she'd read to me about something fun like astronauts or superheroes.

When she finishes, she closes the Bible and smiles at me, which she hardly ever does. Even though it surprises me, I grin back as she asks, "Did you have fun being Clint Eastwood for the night?"

I was dressed up as 'The Man with No Name,' not just Clint Eastwood, but I don't tell her that because my heart is leaping in excitement at her interest in my life. "Yes! I got those new bottle cap candies I've been wanting to try."

Standing, she walks over to pick up my costume off the floor. "Well, that's good. Now, get some sleep."

I listen to her footsteps go down the hall and really do try to do as she says, but I can't stop thinking about all the delicious candy sitting in the pillowcase on the floor. Especially the Bottle Caps. Jerry Cobalt in my class said the root beer ones are the best.

As soon as I hear that she's turned on the shower, I jump out of bed to tip toe across my room and pick up the pillowcase. She'll hear me opening wrappers if she comes to listen by my door. She does that a lot to make sure I'm sleeping. Peeking my head out to find an empty hallway, I close my bedroom door and hurry to the coat closet in the living room. I'll need to see if she's coming, so I decide to keep the door cracked just a little.

Since I don't have much light, I dig through the pillowcase feeling for what I want first. The Bottle Caps must be at the bottom because I can't find them. My fingers wrap around a Nik-L-Nip package, and I decide to just work my way through until I find them. I barely get to suck out the juice when my dad stumbles in, falling into the big chair right in front of me. His bottle sloshes when he slams it on the table, and he mutters under his breath.

I slowly chew on the waxy candy, watching him as he undoes his pants. My eyes go wide when he pulls out his penis, and it sticks straight out. Why is he doing this in the living room? Is he not scared mom will see? He moves his hand fast around it as he starts making weird noises that make my stomach hurt.

Mom will be so mad if she catches him. She beat me with the hair dryer cord so hard my back bled and hurt for days when she saw me touching mine in the bath. I don't understand why it's so bad. I'm too focused on watching my dad to notice my mom until she's screaming from somewhere out of my vision.

"Get out!" He doesn't stop moving his hand.

"That's what you want right? That's why you're drinking and playing with your disgusting little flesh ferret, isn't it?"

"You know what, you fucking cunt? I'm done living with your twisted-ass, psycho bullshit." He slurs as he stands, his wiener still pointing up. I hate him calling her names. "I've tried, Aziza, I really fucking have. In the beginning, I thought I loved you, so waiting until we were married to have you felt worth it. I could understand that." He walks toward her and away from where I can see him through the crack in the door. I'm much too scared to move. I can't even lift my hands to cover my ears. "Then, I find out on our wedding night that you lied to me. You left out the detail that your sick fuck of a father cut up your pussy because you thought I wouldn't marry you if I knew. And maybe I wouldn't have, but as angry as I was at you for keeping that from me, I still understood."

"Don't you dare talk that way about my father! He was a good man. He just wanted me to stay pure! I hear her feet pounding against the floor seconds before she stands where I can see her. "And put that repulsive thing away!"

Suddenly, my father lurches at her, grabbing her

arms and slamming her head on the wall next to me. "You haven't touched me since I put the goddamn kid in you!"

"That's not what it's for! Sex for pleasure is a deplorable sin! I will not tarnish my eternal soul to indulge your perversions," she screams in his face.

He grabs her shoulders to spin her around and push her face against the wall. My father only gets like this when he drinks, otherwise he rarely says a word and definitely isn't violent. It makes my skin burn to see him this way. I wish I was brave like Clint Eastwood. Then I could stop him.

"And yet another thing I wasn't informed of until I was trapped. You've controlled my life for nearly a decade, and I'm fucking done."

My heart beats so hard I'm scared they'll hear it when he lifts up her nightgown and yanks down her underwear. What is he doing?! Streams of tears drench my face when he rubs his penis on her bare bottom, making me cover my mouth so they can't hear me cry.

"NO!" she screams just as his body pushes up hard. He holds her face smashed against the wall. Her crying becomes frantic and scared as her hand grasps at the closet doorframe, right in front of me.

He's hurting her! Why can't I move?

When he leans back, I realize exactly what he's doing...he's putting it into her body. This doesn't make sense. Watching her gasp for breath between sobs makes a sharpness stab my chest. I'm finally able to move enough to reach up and wrap my fingers around hers to hold her hand. Our eyes meet as she squeezes back. I silently promise her I won't let go.

RAG DOLL
Sarah Stein

October 31ˢᵗ ~ Morning

I T'S SO HOT UNDER THIS BLANKET. I'M SWEATING, and the minimal air flow makes it hard to breathe quietly. My body jerks as the car bumps against the road. Is he hitting every dang pothole possible?

Finally, after what has to be at least thirty minutes, the car slows until eventually, it stops. I attempt to even out my breathing, listening to him get out and shuffle around in the trunk. Once it slams shut, I stay in the quiet for what I hope is a sufficient amount of time before sneaking out of the backseat.

The air is chilled, a sweet relief against

my sweaty skin. He has a couple of battery-operated lamps lighting a path for him, and unintentionally, for me. I duck down, hiding behind a tombstone large enough to conceal me while also giving me a clear view of his muscles flexing as he pushes the shovel into the dirt.

I've had a crush on Skeleton King for as long as I can remember. I met him soon after Fink brought me to Hallows Grove when he came over to drop off some supplies for Fink's experiments. Supplies that I now know were most likely just body parts. I'll never forget the way my heart spasmed the first time I laid eyes on him. Back then, he seemed so much older, but he had to have been close to the same age I am now. He wasn't in his makeup that day, allowing me to see every perfect feature. His warm brown hair fell in his face when he tilted his head and stared down at me. His eyes were so dark, they looked like black orbs in a sea of white.

It's been ten years since that day, and my infatuation has only grown. I know his preferences, so it's likely I will never feel him while alive, however, once I muster the courage,

I plan to ask him to be with me when I die.

Watching the great lengths he goes through to be with them makes me terribly angry, though, a different angry than I'm used to. Fink, and even Ingvar, bring out a rage in me that eats away at who I am day by day, yet seeing Skeleton King work so hard for his next corpse bride burns my blood so hot I could scream. What makes them more desirable than me? Besides their death, of course. I don't understand why he wants a girl that can't speak or touch him more than he would want me. I've tried to give him hints over the years with the few chances I've gotten. He either hasn't noticed or isn't interested.

I had no idea how long this was going to take when I stowed away in his car. Not to mention, I didn't account for his dog, Nothing, who I keep expecting to expose me. He never does, though. Part of me wonders if he's keeping the secret of my hiding here. He's such a cute little puppy, and I've always wanted to play with him, but between Fink and Skeleton King, I've either been too nervous or intimidated.

Fink is going to be furious when he realizes I'm gone. He forgot to double check that my door had locked shut again, so after he fell asleep, I took out the little piece of paper I had shoved in the hole to keep it from latching.

Ingvar, Fink's live-in assistant, was much too immersed in eating dog treats and playing Tetris on his Nintendo to notice me sneaking out the front door.

I didn't originally intend on hiding in John's car. I didn't even have a plan, I just wanted to get out of the house for a while, and Hallows Grove is the most interesting during Halloween. While admiring all the clever decorations, I saw him loading up his trunk. On nothing more than a whim, the moment he disappeared into his house, I jumped into his back seat and hid beneath the blanket on the floorboard.

Now, we're clearly outside of Hallows Grove. Since I haven't left the gates for nearly a decade, I'm dying to explore, but my desire to watch him is stronger. The cold air is irritating the scar on my shoulder, so I reach up to massage it. It's been well over a year since Fink removed my right arm simply to reattach it. Just like he does everything else. Since I was a child, he's taken me apart only to put me back together again like a demented puzzle.

I pick the flowers sitting on top of the graves closest to me, making an eclectic bouquet. There's not a lot to do, and admittedly, I nod off a few times through the night until a *thud* startles me from my half sleep. Nothing stares down into the hole that Skeleton King heaves himself out of. Crawling to a smaller, but closer headstone, I kneel to peer around it and watch him. With the shadows from the lanterns dancing on his skin, the haunted beauty of our surroundings, and the poignant effect of his skull-painted face in the moonlight, he appears exactly as his nickname suggests.

A king.

Moments later, after more *thuds* and *bangs*, the body of the girl he's acquiring is lifted from the hole. He climbs out, kneeling next to her. The way he touches her turns my stomach. While I can't hear what he's whispering, I'm sure it's everything I ever wished he'd say to me. There's more light in the sky now, so once he starts laying out the tarp, I'm extra sneaky while I hurry back to his car.

Opening and closing the door as quietly as

possible, I lie on the floorboard behind his seat, concealing myself back under the blanket to wait for him. Time passes so slowly that I take the blanket off a few times just to breathe easier. Finally, I hear him open the trunk and the *thump* of her body being dropped inside.

The car rumbles to life when music and the smell of burning leaves floats around me. As he drives, I smile to myself, listening to the conversation he holds with Nothing.

"What do you want to do tomorrow after I work on Natasha?" Nothing barks, and it's sweet how Skeleton King takes that as a response. "You're overexaggerating. It will not take the entire day. Besides, don't act like you won't be busy with her bones." Nothing whines and John chuckles. "Seriously? Fine, but you can't tell me they don't all taste the same. Besides, the Zeldamines pay the most for pelvic bones, so don't get used to it."

The car stops a few times, making me antsy. It isn't until his door closes that I know we're back at his house. Every time I hear him speak, I get chills that spread like vines across my insides. My hair stands on end, and goosebumps raise across my skin. He's talking to Bolt, I think. Those annoying Sanity Eaters have their nose in everything.

I listen closely for everything to go silent. The triplets' voices trail farther away, and I don't hear Skeleton King anymore. Pushing off the blanket, I look out the window for Nothing before I rush from the car to cross the street. Not a moment too soon either, because just as I turn around, Skeleton King walks out of his front door pushing a stretcher.

He looks up at me with a smile that appears mildly sinister with his smeared face paint. My heart does gymnastics, banging against my ribs so hard, my skin feels on fire. When he acknowledges me with a wave, I think I might burst with how fast my pulse is thumping.

In my nervousness, I forget to wave back, but with my luck already pushed to capacity, I need to hurry home to Fink.

Fink's real name is Franklin. He and Ingvar are the closest thing to family I've had for as long as I can remember. On the rare occasion when I do have any thoughts or memories of the people that might have been my parents, they're always blurry. Fink always says that he 'saved' me. Though, I have no idea from what.

Over the years of being with him, I've deduced that he chose me because of his daughter. I don't know her name because he only calls her his 'pumpkin,' I just know I remind him of her, apparently.

I think he's very sad…so sad that he's confused. In the past ten years, he's taken me apart bit by bit. The first time he cut me was when I was nine. He took off my middle finger and reattached it. I was under anesthesia for the procedure, but when I awoke, fear consumed me in a way I'd never felt before. Once I realized what he had done, I was terribly disoriented. I remember not understanding why he would do that to me if he loved me like he said he did. His stitching was crude and harsh. I know now it's because he wanted me to scar. He wanted my seams to show.

Arriving at the front door, I take in a deep breath. If I'm able to sneak into my room without being noticed, I might get away with my insubordination. If I'm caught, however, I know what the punishment will be.

THE DIRTY HEROES COLLECTION

Vince, my black cat, *purrs* at my feet, rubbing his torso against my leg. Fink gave him to me two years ago. He comes and goes as he pleases, yet always seems to show up when I really need him.

"Hi, Vince," I whisper, kneeling down to pet behind his ears. "Have you had a good night?" Lying on his back, he bats at my hair as I rub his tummy. "I should get inside, you know."

Standing, I attempt to turn the handle, but it's locked. I kneel down to reach into my striped socks for the house key I stole from Fink.

The hinges *creak* as I carefully push open the door and peek my head into the entryway. It's silent, giving me hope that both Fink and Ingvar are still sleeping. I cringe when my boots *knock* loud against the tile.

Looking up the staircase to the mezzanine for any sign of movement, I sigh in relief to find none. The heavy door to my room is loud, but I'm almost home free. *Home free.* That's such a funny saying. Home is the last place that I'm free.

When I switch on my bedroom light, my heart falls, nausea turning it around in my gut.

Fink sits in the chair next to my bed, his fingers tapping his cane. The rage surrounding him is thick in the small room. Ingvar stands in the corner eating a dog biscuit, grinning in a way that suggests the very thing I was trying to avoid is about to happen.

"Fink—"

He *tsks*, shaking his head as he stands unsteadily against his cane. "Do you for some reason enjoy making me angry with you?" He isn't a terribly old man, he's maybe twenty-five years older than me, but his body doesn't match his chronological age. He was in a devastating accident that he refuses to talk about, leaving him with a limp and a large halo-shaped scar around the top of his head. "Where were you this time?" He hobbles toward me, his question obviously a rhetorical one as he continues, "I don't understand why you keep pushing me to these measures. Do you think I take pleasure in having things this way?" He reaches out to caress my cheek. "I despise it. You're hurting us both every time you do this." His head gestures to my twin bed against the wall. "Get undressed and sit with your legs spread."

I wonder if he really believes the lies that drip from his mouth. This would happen whether I snuck out or not, so I may as well get a few hours of independence. It's been years since I've called him 'Dad' like he'd prefer. But I don't really see him that way; he's the warden to my prison. And that bit about him hating this is laughable. The humiliation it puts me through hardens his dick faster than when I suck it.

I could fight. I've done it plenty of times. It's a waste of energy, though, because it's always worse after and never stops anything. Doing as he says, I drop my patchwork dress to the cement floor before removing my socks and boots.

Ingvar finishes his biscuit and unzips his pants, stroking himself as I sit on my bed. "Fuck pussy."

Ingvar only says two- and three-word sentences. I'm not sure what's wrong with him, but what he lacks in brains, he more than makes up for in brawn. I don't think he's actually that much older than me, he's just large.

"That's right, Ingvar. Sarah was a very naughty girl again. I want you to make it hurt, okay?"

Spreading my legs, I rest my heels on the edge of the mattress. Ingvar nods, lowering his pants and stalking toward me with his unsettling grin stretched across his face. He's not an attractive person. At least not to me. Definitely less so than Fink. Licking his lips, he reaches between my legs, rubbing his fat fingers over my entrance. Maybe it's his scent I find so sickening. All I can smell are the dog treats. Suddenly, his giant palm wraps around my throat to push me on my back. The mattress is hard, and as he kneels next to my head, he slaps his erection against my lips. I open my mouth like I'm expected to, immediately feeling the intrusion of him forcing himself down my throat. Gagging around the loose skin of his shaft, I'm stripped of the rest of my oxygen when he squeezes my nostrils closed.

"Sarah suck cock," he moans through heavy breathing.

My lungs are on fire, and just when I think they will explode in my chest, he releases my nose to pull out of my mouth. His hand stays around my neck, though, his grip is mild, allowing me to gasp for air. The oxygen burns my throat, and all I can think about is breathing normally again.

His heavy body weighs down on mine, pushing it deeper into the mattress. Strangled cries fight their way from my mouth when he forces himself into me, stretching and tearing his way inside.

Since sex with Ingvar is a punishment, I'm never allowed to be prepared first. He's entered me dry countless times. When me and Fink are alone, however, he's affectionate and always makes sure I'm aroused.

Ingvar's rancid breath is a hot cloud beneath my nose, making me queasy. He bucks harder into me, grunting while Fink limps to the side of my bed.

Leaning down to kiss me, he brushes the hair from my face. "I don't like doing this, Sarah, but you have to understand. What kind of parent would I be if I didn't give you consequences for your actions?"

I scoff, and his eyes narrow, so I refrain from telling him how sad it is that he truly believes his own lies. With one hand on his cane, he uses his other to undo his slacks and lift my head to meet the tip of his cock. Fink slides slowly between my lips while Ingvar impales me so hard, I'm certain I'll be bruised tomorrow.

Ingvar shudders, his fat belly pushing against me as he empties himself. "Wet. Warm." I'm grateful for the tee shirt he's wearing because I despise the sensation of his skin touching mine.

I've known Ingvar for almost eight years. One day, completely out of the blue, Fink brought him home, saying he was his new apprentice and would be staying with us indefinitely. I tried to be his friend at first, until Fink began using him to punish me. I've always wondered what he really thinks of me. Obviously, he doesn't say much, and he's clearly loyal to Fink. It's just that sometimes I get the notion he hates me.

"Clean her up," Fink orders, pumping his hips a few times before removing himself from between my lips and backing away to sit in the chair.

Every time Ingvar fucks me, Fink makes him eat me out afterward and won't have sex with me until he does. Ingvar's hands squeeze my waist, lifting me into the air before tossing my legs over his shoulders. My bare butt touches his T-shirt as my thighs rub against his ears.

He lifts up my ass, forcing me to hold on to his head for balance. Smashing my clit against his mouth, he licks and slurps, tasting me inside and out.

It confuses me why Fink allows this. Ingvar knows my body and can make me orgasm almost as quickly as Fink can. I don't know why he would let me have the pleasure. I look over at Fink's darkened expression, bucking my hips as I forfeit to the building arousal. If he truly hates seeing me with Ingvar as he claims, then I will have a hand in his torment. Without looking away from him, I ride Ingvar's tongue, pulling his hair until the tightness spreads over my skin, about to snap like a rubber band.

I move faster and faster. The liquid is coming. I break eye contact with Fink the same moment I'm shoved over the brink. It floods out of me, filling Ingvar's mouth and rolling over his cheeks. I can't stop my moans while it sprays down his neck, drenching his shirt.

My chest heaves, and my legs shake against his shoulders. While I hate that this is how I have to achieve it, orgasms are easily the best feeling I've ever experienced. Ingvar throws me on the bed, sucking my nipples with his wet lips.

"You can go, Ingvar. We'll meet in the lab later." Without even getting dressed, he obeys, picking up his pants and leaving my room. I take in deep breaths, preparing myself for the second part of my punishment.

Fink sees it as us 'making up' after I've gotten in trouble. His cane *taps* against the concrete on his way back to my bed. Sitting next to me, he sighs as he unbuttons his lab coat. "I know you want more freedom, Sarah." His shoes and socks are dropped to the floor before he reaches out to brush his fingers across my cheek. "If anything happened to you, I don't know if I could deal with it. I'm simply trying to protect you."

He's always more lenient on me during these moments. I think he truly believes these times between us are special. When I was younger, I thought they were too. As scary as it was, it made him so happy, and I wanted nothing more than to please him.

"I feel like I'm losing my mind locked up

in here all the time! You always say that I'm not ready...will I ever be ready?"

After he's fully undressed, he settles between my legs, pressing gentle kisses all over my face. "I need you to trust me. All I'm doing is keeping you safe." He slides into me with ease, each thrust slow and gentle. He whispers, "Daddy loves his rag doll."

Oddly, his words strike up the memory of when I first learned that this was how babies were made. When I read about it in one of his books, the very idea had been so exciting to me. I would finally have someone to play with.

"Dad! Dad! Am I going to have a baby? Look!" I run into his lab, holding my hand against my chest because it's still healing from the reattachment procedure. Showing the book to him, I read the sentence that got me excited. "During sexual intercourse, semen is ejaculated from the penis into the woman's vagina where it is then possible for the sperm to fertilize the woman's egg." He doesn't look up from his telescope. "So? How long until I have one?" Is he even paying attention? "Dad!"

Dropping his head back, he groans as he removes

his glasses. *"You won't ever have babies, Sarah. I took care of that the first year you were here. You're as empty as a Russian doll at a thrift store."* He waves me off, holding his hand out for the slide Ingvar is holding. *"Now go to your room. I have work to do."*

His response pulls tears from my eyes. *"What do you mean, 'took care of it?'"*

Narrowing his eyebrows, he pushes up on shaky legs. *"I cut it all out. I brought you here for you only. I have no desire to have more children. You are the only child I need."*

I've been angry and hurt by him many times, but this feels different. It was unfair of him to take that chance away from me. And then for him to act as if what he did was okay. Ingvar smirks as the book gets heavy in my hand with the urge to throw it at my dad's head. I stop myself, though, because if I do that, he'll lock me up for days.

On my way back to my bedroom, I look out the window seeing the garden in the backyard. He's only showed it to me once, telling me which plants I should never touch. He said the pretty ones that look like purple bells and black marbles could make me very sick or even kill me. Looking over my shoulder to make sure they're both still in the lab, I sneak *outside.*

There are big scissors and garden gloves in the greenhouse so I grab them both before kneeling in front of the plant I'm looking for. Belladonna. *It's such a pretty name for something that could do such terrible things. I don't know how much I need, so I cut off three black orbs, sliding them into the pocket of my dress. The next time he asks me to make his tea, I will make him pay for what he did.*

I got scared of what would happen to me if he died, so in the end, I only ended up using one berry. He was messed up for days, having convulsions and hallucinations that terrified me. When he regained his strength, he knew what I had done and was more furious with me than he had ever been before. That was the first time he let Ingvar fuck me.

Fink moans my name as he quickens his thrusts, moments later filling me up and panting into my neck. We're both covered in sweat by the time it's finally over. As he gets dressed, he says, "Take a shower, and then make me some breakfast. If you're good, I'll let you stay up with Ingvar tonight to watch the fireworks."

Every year I beg to go to the Halloween Games, and every year he says 'no.'

I ask anyway. "Can't I go this year? *Please*?"

His head drops back in frustration as he turns on my music box. He knows the angelic tune relaxes me. The porcelain couple dance in a circle while he says, "Why do you keep asking questions that make me the bad guy? I just told you, you're not ready yet."

Even as I nod, I decide I'm not missing it again this year. He won't expect me to push my luck by sneaking out again so soon, plus it's been a while since I resorted to using Belladonna, since I don't have much left. He hid the plant, so all I have is what I've stockpiled in my room and in the kitchen.

I do as he says, taking a shower and putting on the T-shirt he has me wear when my dress is being cleaned. As I toss my dress into the washing machine, I notice a rip in the fabric. I'll need to add another patch to it. After I throw in some of Fink and Ingvar's clothes, I go to the kitchen to make his oatmeal. In the very back of the cabinet behind the canned food and dried rice, sits the jar hiding the Belladonna. My heart races with excitement as I cut off a small portion of the berry.

Happy Halloween to me.

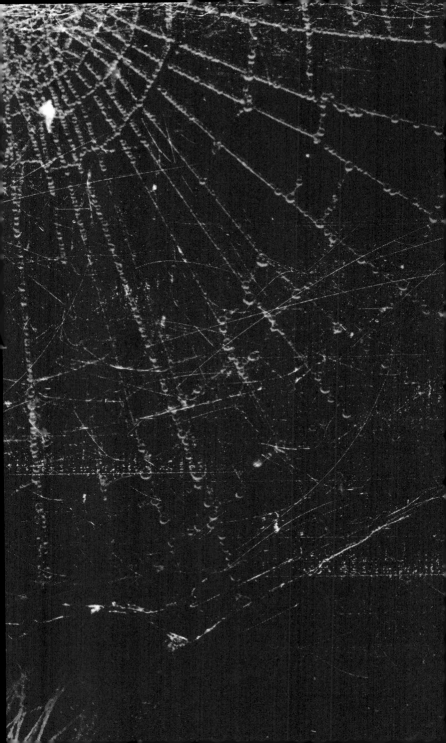

HALLOWEEN GAMES
John Skelver

October 31st ~ Evening

"YOU'RE SO DAMN TIGHT."
My fingers dig into the dead flesh of her ass cheeks as I thrust into her small hole. The room is bright with the mid-day sun which allows me to see every mark and blemish on her ashen skin. She's on her stomach, arm dangling off the side of the bed while her hair curls across the pillow. Her white eyes look vacantly toward my dresser and I try not to breathe too deeply. Her smell is getting stronger and will be worse by the time I get back. She'll need another bath.

I buck my hips harder, feeling the dense pressure rising. My moan is loud in the quiet room as my come spurts into her corpse.

Shuddering with the final jolts of my orgasm, I slide out of her cadaver and leave her in my bed. I never showered last night, so I walk to the bathroom to wash off the cemetery dirt and face paint. Just knowing she'll be here waiting for me tonight will make the games less tedious. Not that they aren't entertaining, they've just become a tiresome affair.

Shortly after I first came here, my habits were simply preferences, and people found them charming. I loved their enthusiasm at first. I was a teenage outcast, and their acceptance helped patch up my self-esteem and nurture my confidence. I will always owe this town for that. I'd made friends with the residents fairly easily. I had wanted so badly to be liked, I did anything and everything asked of me. Mostly simple things, like helping the Zeldamine sisters mend their roof, or watching the Bognar triplets as toddlers. Even now, if I'm asked a favor, I'll usually do it.

It wasn't until Fink asked me to dig up a body for him that I suddenly became the town's main source of body parts. Before me, they all

THE DIRTY HEROES COLLECTION

had to fend for themselves to find what they needed. I went from just digging up girlfriends to digging up inventory, morphing me into a god.

It's actually quite interesting how many uses there are for a human corpse. Wanda and Willow Zeldamine, the old sisters two streets over, use the skin to make curtains and bed skirts, the bones to make furniture and tableware, and almost everything else for their apothecary business. Sometimes, Bone Daddy, a local jazz musician, will buy teeth from me because his wife makes jewelry or grinds them up, adding dyes to create makeup. There's Kline Mitchem, an acquaintance of mine who works as a traveling performer in a gothic clown show. He'll sometimes purchase face skin to turn into masks. The town's fortune teller, Madame Emerald, prefers the arm, leg, and rib bones because she transforms them into sex toys that she sells at craft fairs around the state.

Those are some of my regular clients, though, I get quite a few random orders too. Regardless of the customer, they pay well for what they buy, plus I also make a fairly steady income from my taxidermy business. I get decent exposure from the ads I put in newspapers, but word of mouth is my best source of advertising.

I'm tired, though. There's a need inside me that I can't meet because I don't know what it is. Every year that passes, the mass of emptiness in my soul seems to burrow deeper. I've always felt there was something separating me from everyone else. I had thought that 'something' was my necro-romanticism, but the longer the clock of time ticks away, I become more aware that there's something else I'm missing.

Nothing sleeps on my bed next to Natasha while I pull on my black and white pin-striped pants. "Did you eat your food?" I ask, sitting next to him to tug on my black boots. "We slept all day. We'll be leaving for the games soon, and I won't give you a single pig in a blanket if your food isn't gone." As if sulking, he releases a soft growl and slowly leaves my room.

"Crazy-ass dog," I laugh toward the direction of Natasha who obviously doesn't respond.

After grabbing a white T-shirt from my top drawer, I walk to the kitchen to make coffee.

Nothing is chomping on the meat I skimmed for him from my last body. I mix it with peas which he's not a fan of, but I try to balance his diet.

Boiling a couple of eggs, I make toast and pour my coffee before carrying it all back to the bedroom, relaxing beside Natasha while reading my newest book.

The games have become exhausting the last few years. Everyone wants something from me, even if it's only my time. There are days when I fantasize about leaving and starting over elsewhere, left alone in solitude. I could never leave here, though. It's my home, plus there's not a single place I know of where I could live this freely.

Maybe I'm just in a rut.

Lighting a joint, I kiss Natasha before walking to the bathroom to get ready. I clip back the strands around my hairline to protect it from the greasepaint. While it may seem somewhat cliché, painting my face like a skull not only hides my identity while grave robbing, it also makes me feel safe and has become a staple of how people see me.

With a white eyeliner pencil, I outline the

circles around my eyes and accentuate the bones on my cheeks, nose, and forehead. Right on schedule, Nothing walks in, lying on the rug to watch me as I use black grease paint to shape the skull, darkening the space next to the hairline.

When I put on the paint, it's as if I become someone else. The moment the skull is on my face, I transform from John Skelver to Skeleton King.

I finish with the highlights and details, setting it all by covering a velour puff with translucent powder and dabbing it on top of the paint. Waiting a few minutes to allow it to dry, I sweep off the excess powder with the human hair bristle brush Kline gave me and begin styling my hair.

I choose a white button-down shirt and roll up the sleeves as I look for my signature, black bow tie.

"Where is that fucking thing?" Nothing whines behind me, making me shake my head with a laugh when I see he's carrying it in his mouth. "Thanks, boy." I toss on a vest and lean over the bed, kissing Natasha. "I'll see you tonight." Patting my leg, I call over my shoulder. "Come on, Nothing. It's time to go."

He rushes past me, tail wagging as he waits by the door. Ogier Bognar's house is only a couple streets over, and it isn't too cold tonight, so I opt to walk. Even though the games don't officially start for forty-five minutes, I always have to come early for photographs.

The mayor has already arrived when I reach Ogier's tall, three-story house at the corner of the intersection. Honestly, I'm annoyed by him half of the time, but Mayor Greer's family is the reason this place exists. His great-great grandfather founded Hallows Grove. As the story goes, he got a thrill from hunting humans for sport, but when he had a close call with the authorities, he began to draw up the plans for Hallows Grove. He ran with a rough crowd which consisted of those who are now known as the founding families. Together, they purchased the land that Hallows Grove sits on, and over the past one hundred years, this place has grown into a mostly self-sufficient community.

We have our own way of doing things here. There was never an election for Mayor Greer;

he simply took over when his father passed, like he had done after his father before him. The Hallows Grove police are more like the mayor's henchman than actual law enforcement. As residents, we're all able to voice our opinions and speak freely, though, ultimately, Mayor Greer and the town council have the last word. There aren't many laws, however, those that are in place are there to protect us all and are strictly enforced. Truthfully, it's what works for us.

Walking into the multi-use building behind Ogier's house, I'm somehow still in awe at the level of detail in the décor. I swear, it gets better every year. Coffin shaped tables and spider web streamers stretch across the dining area. Drinks are served in cauldrons, and lit jack-o'-lanterns hang from the ceiling. I scan the blackjack, poker, and craps tables lined up in front of the slot machines. Game and food booths are set up along the walls with merchant tables scrunched in between. The Halloween Games are run like a mix between a festival and a casino, which isn't surprising since that's what Ogier does for a living. He owns DarkSide, a casino located in the Mundane World, making him the richest man in Hallows Grove.

"John! Welcome, welcome! Come over here!" Mayor Greer holds his hands up in greeting.

I never know what I'm going to get with him. There are times he's so joyful it's contagious, and others when he'll rip your throat out for blinking in his direction.

He pats me on the back as he leads me over to Ogier, holding one of his whores on a leash as the triplets taunt her with a slingshot. Members of the town council and other local political officials mingle alongside Madame Emerald's fortune telling booth.

I lift my hand in greeting to Ogier as he grins at me. "Ah, Skeleton King! Now the night can officially begin." He yanks on the leash causing the girl at the end of it to choke. "The kids told me you acquired a new lady friend this morning. Congratulations."

My arrogance wishes I would have taken a Polaroid of her before I left so I could show off her loveliness. A proud smile crawls up my face. "Her name is Natasha. She's quite the beauty."

Ogier doesn't have time to respond before

Mayor Greer snaps, "It's time to take the fucking pictures. Stand in a row and smile, for Christ's sake." Frowning, he positions us for the local photographer. It isn't long before town residents start pouring in, lining up for their personal photo with me in front of the dripping blood backdrop.

I really don't know why they worship me as much as they do. Part of me is grateful for their acceptance, while the other part just wishes they'd leave me to my own devices. It can be draining. Thankfully, tonight is when their gushing reaches its peak. It started because I used to bring a body to the games, performing the first few stages of taxidermy for their enjoyment. It was a lot of work, though, and eventually became something I preferred to do privately. Now, I think I've become more of a symbol than anything else.

Finally, after what feels like I've posed for hundreds of pictures, the crowd expands to enjoy the festivities of the evening. My eyes travel through the game players, looking for Fink. It's odd that he isn't here. Since he's a descendant of one of the founding families, it's assumed he'll attend the biggest event of the year.

I win a couple hundred dollars playing blackjack and watch Kline trying his hand at the knife throwing competition. We play that a little differently here. The point is to get as close to the target as possible without actually hitting it. The target this year is a man I've never seen before, and I'm assuming he's one of the whores Ogier bought for the evening. The Bognar family has always dealt in the sex trade, giving Ogier easy access to what he sees as disposable bodies.

The man is fastened to a large, spinning wheel and appears high out of his mind, barely reacting when the knife Kline throws lands in his arm.

"Damn it," Kline squeals in the high-pitched voice he takes on whenever he's in his clown persona.

I'm nearly knocked over as a group of kids run toward the movie room. It's actually a pretty neat set up. Horror films are played on a large, white wall via a projector that Ogier purchased last year from a theater in the Mundane World that was going out of business.

I follow them and lean against the wall to watch for a few minutes. From what I can tell, the film currently showing is about a freaky, red-haired, apparently possessed doll, who's running around with a knife, tormenting a little boy and his mom. On my way out, I snatch up one of the little pumpkin buckets of popcorn before returning to the games.

While stopping to chat with the Zeldamine sisters at their booth, I admire a lampshade made of skin that came from at least four different bodies. The swirled needlepoint designs are so intricate and stunning, I consider purchasing it for myself.

A high-pitched laugh catches my attention, causing me to glance toward the whore lounge. The curtains are cracked open wide enough that if I got closer, I would be able to clearly see inside.

Waving to the sisters, I make my way to the lounge, stopping before crossing the threshold.

I wrap my fingers around the velvet curtain, my eyes landing on a young woman, adorning a collar and chains. She gags while police chief, Baron Vendire, violently shoves his cock down her throat. Her hips rock back to meet the thrusts of the other Vendire brother, Lestar. I can't help imagining what her pussy feels like as I watch the brothers use her for their pleasure.

Ogier walks up next to me, slapping my back. "Want to try your hand at a girl that can actually suck your dick? No trick, it's my treat."

She doesn't look like she's suffering, but that doesn't necessarily mean she wants to be here. A lot of things about this town shocked and even repulsed me at first, and I suppose they still do, I've just become used to them. That doesn't mean I have to involve myself any more than required. I'm not a rapist. If I were, I wouldn't need the dead girls. Regardless of that, I'm not stupid enough to accept anything Ogier offers. I don't trust him and never will.

"That's generous, but I must humbly decline." I turn away from his hand on my back and walk toward the bar. "Enjoy the games."

"Suit yourself." He shrugs before stepping behind the curtain.

When the night is more than half over and the excitement begins to die down, Mayor Greer announces the raffle and auction winners over the speaker.

"First up, is this massive gift basket from Zeldamine Apothecary."

With everyone's attention on the raffle, I pat my leg for Nothing to follow me, slipping out the back doors before the fireworks start.

The nip in the air is revitalizing as I walk down the empty street. I want to go home, so I can't explain why I continue farther into town. Natasha is waiting for me, so why am I walking away from her?

Although Hallows Grove cemetery hasn't had a new body buried in it in years, it's a peaceful place to me. Graveyards are my playground, my safe place. Nothing runs between the aging plots as I sit in front of the largest headstone, the one belonging to Mayor Greer's great-great grandfather. Flipping open my Zippo, I pull a joint from my pocket, watching the end glow orange once it's lit.

The smoke is gray in the moonlight as I rest my head against the hard granite. Nothing sniffs his way around and I enjoy the silence. Suddenly, his attention is drawn to a certain gravestone causing him to bark into the darkness.

"Whatcha messin' with, boy?"

He doesn't acknowledge me, so I take a long drag while standing to see what has him so interested.

I hear a soft, "Shush, buddy," before I see her. Cute, little, redheaded Sarah Stein. What exactly is she doing? I know Fink would never let her out, tonight of all nights. Her irises, that are abnormally small, lift to mine, her eyes wide with what I think is fear.

"I-I um…" She won't meet my gaze, and I instantly wonder if she's hurt.

Kneeling in front of her, I ask, "Are you all right?"

Her hair falls in her face as she looks to the ground.

"I just…" Shifting her eyes back up to meet my stare, she shakes her head. "I don't want to go home yet. Fink is already…mad." She reaches out to me before snapping her hand back. "Please don't tell him I'm here."

The sound of desperation in her voice makes my ribcage feel like it's being crushed together. I'll admit, I have a special relationship with Franklin 'Fink' Stein. He's the reason I even live here. When I was sixteen, I met a mortician that allowed me 'privacy' with the cadavers for a certain price. That bastard was a crook. At the time, Fink was paying him for organs to use in his experiments. We met in passing one day, and after an awkward conversation along with a cup of coffee, I found myself getting a tour of the place I now call home.

Fink was actually the first person I'd ever felt a real human connection with. Because of that, I've turned a blind eye to what he's doing with Sarah. I've forced myself to ignore it because it's less uncomfortable than confronting him. Not to mention, it's illegal here to put any type of shame or judgement on a Hallows Grove resident. That doesn't make it feel any less wrong, though. I may have a pit in my soul, but it isn't hollowed out completely.

"Your secret's safe with me. I promise." Reaching out, I take her hand, feeling the bumps of scars that I know tatter her youthful flesh. The warmth radiating from her is so jarring I almost jerk my hand away. I'm so used to the cold. I help her to her feet as a sweet smile lifts her full lips. Quickly separating our hands, I hold the joint out to her. "You want some?"

She shrugs and takes it. "Sure." My eyebrow quirks at the huge hit she inhales. Almost instantly, she doubles over in a coughing fit. "What is that?" The words fight to come out in between her hacking.

"It's only weed," I laugh, earning me a frown.

Shoving it in my face, she coughs one more time. "Thanks, but I don't want this."

I bring it to my lips, taking a drag of my own. "Fair enough. Would you like to walk with me?" Nothing makes his way deeper into the cemetery while sniffing everything in his path.

The big smile lifting her cheeks transforms her features, somehow making her even more beautiful. "Okay." The wind blows her hair across her face as we pass more worn headstones. "Why are you out here anyway? Shouldn't Skeleton King be inside at the games?"

This is probably the longest conversation we've ever had. It's also the most pleasant I've ever felt in the presence of a breathing woman. I'm shocked at myself when the words I've only spoken to Nothing and the dead pour from my lips.

"Sometimes it can be so...unfulfilling." It's invigorating yet terrifying to confess this to someone with the ability to repeat it. "Everyone sees me as this," I gesture to my painted face, "but I just want to be John."

"Do you...do you ever think about leaving?" Her voice takes on a higher octave, breaking on the last word.

Tilting my head back and forth, I consider how to respond. It's more complicated than that. Skeleton King is part of who I am.

"Occasionally, but to where? You know who I am. I wouldn't be welcome in the Mundane World."

She sighs in what feels like relief. As she turns to face me, the moonlight shines across her soft features, creating a tingle beneath my skin. When she meets my eyes, her heated hand wraps around mine, and I suck in a breath at the sensation. "Maybe you could just stop?" Shaking her head, she stutters, "B-being Skeleton King, I mean."

Her words are kind, however impossible. The only thing I can think about is her touching me. I can't tear my stare away from our hands. Right as I open my mouth to try to speak, Fink's pained voice carries through the graveyard.

"Sarah! Sarah! I know you're out here! Get your fucking ass home right now!"

The *whistle* of the first firework being shot off shrieks in the distance. Orange lights explode in the sky above us as her eyes widen. "I gotta go," she whispers, dropping my hand and running away, taking her heat with her.

SMILE

Sarah Stein

October 31ˢᵗ ~ Night

MY HEART THRASHES IN MY CHEST WHILE MY smile sits permanently on my face. He was so nice, and we touched hands! Twice! Whatever Fink does to me will be worth the last few minutes. I take the long way, which means he'll beat me home, but at least it will delay the inevitable.

Vince is sprawled on the doorstep when I arrive. "Hi, kitty," I whisper. "Is Fink back yet?"

He *meows*, and I sigh, bracing myself to go inside. Fink is standing in the entryway, glaring at me when I step through the door. I don't even get it closed before Ingvar grabs my shoulders, squeezing me tight with my back against his chest. I grunt, failing at my attempt to push against his arms.

Fink stalks toward us, his cane *knocking* against the floor with each step as he seethes, "Do you want me dead? Is that it?"

I push my shoulders against Ingvar's chest and stop fighting. "Of course not. You're being silly."

"Silly?!" he yells. "You know how lethal Belladonna is! You're lucky it hasn't killed me already!"

'Lucky' isn't the word that comes to mind. "Then maybe you should make your own food," I snap.

He straightens against his cane with narrowed eyes. "Bring her to the lab, Ingvar."

Tossing me over his shoulder like a sack of potatoes, Ingvar carries me upstairs where he straps me to a table in Fink's laboratory.

"Still," he orders.

I can hear Fink's cane *tap*, *tap*, *tapping* as he makes his way into the lab. He chooses his implements as Ingvar cleans my cheeks. I know what that means. My face is going to be cut.

"Do you know your importance, Sarah? Really?" Fink shuffles around for the implements he'll need, his back to me as he speaks. "I left Hallows Grove when I began attending college. There, I met my ex-wife, and we started a family, living a peaceful, mundane life. But when our daughter died, I couldn't fathom a life without my child."

Ingvar tilts the table, leaving me at a forty-five-degree angle and giving me a better view of Fink.

"I was working at a prestigious university at the time, researching the possibilities of cloning. The moment my daughter took her last breath, I knew exactly what I needed to do. Though her body was difficult to acquire, once I had it, I used the school's funding and equipment in an attempt to bring her back. Unfortunately, before I was successful, I was caught, losing my wife and my career in the process." The implements *clank* on the surgical table as Fink lays them out in a row. "Shortly after that, my father passed away, and with nowhere else to go, I came back here to take my rightful place on the town council."

His chilled fingers brush the hair from my cheeks before cupping my chin. The blue irises in his eyes move back and forth as he examines my face. "A few years later, I saw you for the first time. In that moment, I knew you were worthy to serve as the representation of her. Having you with me is a passable substitute for the daughter I lost." Sliding the needle into a glass bottle, he fills it with the clear liquid. The lidocaine syringe drips as he taps the barrel and asks, "Are you happy here?"

I snort as Ingvar breathes so heavily next to me that I can smell the dog biscuits he eats all the time. "I'm absolutely blissful."

Fink frowns, leaning down to inject me with the numbing agent. "Sarcasm is unbecoming on a woman. As is the lack of a smile." The needle slides out of my left cheek before it's inserted into my right. "I miss your smile, Sarah."

Once the lidocaine kicks in, I don't know if I'll be able to speak. It's only been recently that he's opened up to me about his past, so I want to ask my question before I'm unable to.

"Why do you do this to me? Cut me up? Why wouldn't you want me whole?"

A small smile curves his lips. "You are many things to me. A daughter, a lover—but you're also a symbol and a reminder. My pumpkin's name was Sarah, and she loved dolls... Rag dolls specifically."

His words sink in, allowing me to process what he said. Sarah...that isn't my real name. It's hers. The revelation has me shuffling through my brain, trying to remember what I might have been called before coming here.

The lower part of my face tingles, like my jaw is being dissolved, taking away my ability to speak.

"You encompass all of that, and I will work on you until I believe you're complete. You are my ultimate experiment. The problem is, my pumpkin was always a happy girl, yet you've become so sour. Maybe if you look like you're smiling, someday you'll feel it again for real."

These procedures and amputations used to terrify me. Now I've grown fairly accustomed to them and have accepted that this is my fate. He picks up a Sharpie to mark my face. Remaining silent, he soon trades the marker for a scalpel.

Thick pressure pushes against my cheek

as Fink gives me the smile he spoke of. Bright red soaks the gauze cloth once he lifts it from the wound and takes the large needle threaded with polyester suture from Ingvar.

"Is clean." Ingvar says as he holds up a rectangular mirror.

Having to actually look at the mutilation always makes it worse. Considering I've seen my detached limbs next to me on a table before, I don't understand why this is making my heartrate speed up so fast.

Leaning over me, Fink holds the side of my mouth as he punctures the split flesh with the needle. Although I can't feel any real pain, there's a definite sensation of tugging as he ties off the first stitch. He works his way up, snipping the thread each time, leaving little black strings sticking out of my face.

"You hurt me tonight, Sarah. I'm not only physically ill, but my heart is broken over the fact that you could do that to me. I saved you, done nothing besides love you and care for you, yet you repay me with disobedience and violence."

He repeats the process with my other cheek,

and I wish he'd go a little faster. As ugly as the stitching is, seeing the gaping gash in my face is much worse. After administering morphine through an IV, he softly rubs his hand over my hair. It's always intrigued me that he tries to make this as comfortable as possible, even when he's angry at me.

He unbuckles me from the table, following Ingvar as he carries me down to my room. Once I'm in my bed and Ingvar leaves, he says, "You know I'm trying to protect you, don't you? There are people that could hurt you, or take you from me. I can't bear the thought of something happening to you."

Even knowing his words are sincere, they don't really make sense considering he does what he does to me. His broken mind blurs his obsession with his true emotions. I hate him so much sometimes, yet other times, I think he's just trying to stop the pain.

My skin starts to feel fuzzy as my body loosens and relaxes. "Hmmm." This is the only good part of these surgeries. When the meds kick in. For a few minutes, I feel too amazing to care about much of anything.

"You need to rest tonight, so we'll complete your punishment tomorrow. Sleep well, my little rag doll."

Lifting the blankets to my shoulders, he kisses my forehead and turns on my music box. Without another word, he shuts off the light, leaving me to be lulled into a drug induced sleep.

November 1st ~ Evening

ONE THING ABOUT FINK IS THAT HE ALWAYS KEEPS his promises. I'm left alone in my room without any company besides the meals slid through the slot in my door.

It isn't until the following night that my door opens again. Fink walks over to me, taking my hand without saying a word. While he appears calm, the heat of his fury floats from his skin.

He leads me to the laboratory where Ingvar waits, his cock already tenting his pants with his arousal. "I don't know why you continue to make choices that force me into these things, but I will not be the kind of father that doesn't follow through."

I'm not sure if it will hurt to speak, so I don't give him the satisfaction of more than a glare for my response. Ingvar walks over to me, his fat hands lifting my patchwork dress over my head. I stand there naked for what seems like ages before Fink unbuttons his lab coat and lowers the zipper on his pants.

"Let's see how much you've healed. Come here."

My mouth is so dry that I swallow on my way to meet him. Falling to my knees, I become nauseated by the fear rolling around in my stomach. This is going to be terribly painful. All I can hope for is that he'll let me stop before it becomes too agonizing. His cock looks bigger now that I know I'll have to fit it into my bloody, sore mouth.

"Take it slow," Fink orders.

I stroke his erection, delaying the inevitable for as long as possible. Looking up at him, I beg him with my eyes to not make me do this.

He denies me with a nod of his head.

With a deep breath through my nose, I

slowly open my mouth. Instantly, the threading pulls, sending sharp jabs across the sides of my cheeks. I instinctively back away when Fink grabs my neck, shaking his head as he *clicks* his tongue.

He presses his soft tip to my lips, and I attempt to slurp it into my mouth like gelatin. Tears fall down my face, burning the incisions as he pushes himself deeper. I cry around his erection when he pumps hard three times. My cheeks are ripping apart, and I can feel blood dripping down my jaw when he says, "That's enough for today, we'll try again tomorrow."

My entire face is on fire, and it takes all my self-control to not reach up and touch it. He pushes down his pants, dropping them to the floor before sitting in the nearest chair and resting his cane against the cabinets. He summons me with a wave of his hand.

"Come over here and sit on Daddy."

I do as he says, straddling him and holding onto his shoulders for support. Without wasting time, I slide down his cock, rolling my hips, hoping an orgasm will distract me from the pain in my face. A droplet of blood falls from my jaw, splattering across his white lab coat when I rock my body faster.

"Fuck, Sarah. That's such a good girl." Fink drops his head back and moans.

The doorbell's eerie *ring* reverberates in my ear as Fink gestures to Ingvar, whose erection protrudes in his pants, to answer the door.

I move my body faster, trying to make him come so I can get this over with and go back to bed. Then I hear it. *His* voice. Even with shame suffocating me, I look to the doorway where he stands with Nothing next to his feet. He's seen me in compromising positions before, but after the night of the Halloween Games, I'm horrified.

Adding to my mortification, Fink pumps fast beneath me, pushing my hips back and forth. "Ah, John, my boy. What brings you here today?"

Fink smacks my ass, and I can't help thinking he's making a show of this. Whether it's to impress John or embarrass me, I have no idea.

John—which I am making it a point to call him now instead of Skeleton King—isn't wearing his skull face. It's just him in all his gorgeous glory. His nose is the cutest thing I've ever seen, and the face paint completely distorts that.

"I, um…" His arm bulges in his shirt as he rubs the back of his neck, attempting to divert his gaze, until he can't anymore and it meets mine. "I was hoping to borrow some equipment…and ask your opinion on a few things."

More than anything, I wish I knew what he was thinking. He just stares while Fink fucks me so hard that I can't stop the moans falling from my bloody lips. More tears drip down my face, though, this time it's not from pain, it's from humiliation.

"Of course, you needn't even ask." Fink's hands lift me up, spreading my butt cheeks apart. "Her ass is begging to be fucked. Would you like to try?" Oh, this is definitely to impress John. He's never shared me with anyone other than Ingvar. I wish I could disappear into dust. It's surprising how much I'm hoping that he doesn't agree. I don't want the first time I'm with him to be with Fink or anyone for that matter. Whether I'm breathing or not. "Unless you'd like your privacy? I'll allow it for my dear friend, Skeleton King."

My heart bounces in my chest when suddenly, my desires flip. In my mind, I desperately plead with him to accept. I've always dreamed of him with my dead body, touching and kissing it. To be able to be alive to feel that? The excitement is almost too much to bear.

I'm going to die if the silence lasts much longer. I want nothing more than to see his face right now. Is he considering it? Repulsed? Aroused?

His awkward chuckle hollows out my gut. "You're very generous, really, but I just want to get started on some experiments."

Questions as to why he refused drown my thoughts. Is it because I breathe air or because I'm ugly and scarred? Fink smacks my thigh. "Get up and bend over." On shaky legs, I stand to lean over the cabinets. As he steadies against me, Fink lines himself up, shoving back inside before telling John, "I'll be done in a moment, feel free to look around for what you need in the meantime."

Keeping my eyes squeezed shut, I listen to John and Nothing's footsteps walking around the lab. The *tinkling* of jars accompanies the sound of Fink's grunts in my ear. Finally, he jerks behind me, emptying himself as he moans, "Yes, that's my tight, little rag doll." As he pulls out of me, he spanks my rear. "Get dressed."

I refuse to look at John. Kneeling down, I pick up my dress as his words freeze me solid.

"Hi, Sarah."

Moving feels impossible, so I attempt to even out my breathing before I meet his gaze. His mouth is quirked halfway into a smile, revealing the dimple on his left cheek, but the way his eyes are narrowed makes him look almost angry. "H-hi."

"Ingvar, put Sarah in her room while I help John," Fink orders.

Rushing away from all three of them, I put myself in my room. A moment later, my door *clicks* locked, and I turn on my music box, falling back on my bed with a groan.

It was so close to happening. I could have felt the only touch I've ever dreamed about. Why did he say no? It's going to drive me insane to wonder. Not that knowing would make me any less sad.

While it's true, I've fantasized about him since the day we met, it was mostly pure and innocent in the beginning. I'll never forget the first time I realized that I also wanted him sexually.

"Dad, it wasn't me! I promise! It was him," I scream as I look at Ingvar, trying to pull myself free from his grip. "Tell him, Ingvar!"

Ingvar grins at me in his hateful way, continuing to drag me through the living room. He did it to get me in trouble. I know it.

"Keep lying, Sarah, and this will be much worse. Why would Ingvar break an entire shelf of beakers?"

"Why do you think? So you'll make him fuck me again!"

Fink backhands me before jerking me away from Ingvar. "You won't guilt me out of punishing you. Your actions have consequences. A lesson you still refuse to learn."

He shoves me to my knees, making them rub against the scratchy rug as he squeezes my shoulder. "You know the lab is off limits unless I'm in there with you. You deliberately disobeyed that rule, destroying my equipment and lying to my face." Why doesn't he believe me? "I think you need to start by apologizing to Ingvar." He nods to him. "Go ahead, my boy."

Ingvar stalks toward me, grinning as he takes down his overalls. "Open mouth." Stepping out of the denim, he rubs the extra skin he has over his penis. Fink's doesn't look like that.

"Kiss ass," I say, mocking his tone.

He brings his fist back, landing it so hard against my face that black flashes across my eyes as I fall to the floor.

"Ingvar! Hit her that hard one more time and you will never participate in her punishment again."

Ingvar actually looks ashamed, his eyes shiny with tears as he nods his head. "Yes, sir."

Fink walks over to me, snapping his fingers. "Stand up." As soon as I obey, he grips my chin hard. "I don't know where this attitude of yours has been coming from, but it's not the least bit amusing." He releases me so hard, my head jerks to the side. "Now, get back on your knees."

Sighing in defeat, I kneel on the floor where Ingvar meets me, hard erection in hand. I continue to glare at him as I do what I'm supposed to. He thrusts his disgusting cock into my mouth, yanking at my hair and smacking the back of my head with his *palm. When his pace gets harder and faster, I can't do anything except try to breathe.*

Finally, he pushes me away, allowing me a couple minutes to gasp for air before picking me up to toss me over the edge of the sofa. My fingernails scratch at the fabric as a scream rips through my throat when It feels like he tears open the tight ring of my butt. I hear him grunting, but all I feel is burning pain. Fink is blurry through my tears when the doorbell rings and I look up at him.

He doesn't give Ingvar any instructions when he leaves to answer the door. Sobbing into the couch, I gasp out my question. "Why did you do this?" Ingvar's only response is him thrusting harder. "I've tried to be nice to you! Why can't we be friends?"

"Fuck Sarah."

I don't know exactly what he means by that, but it doesn't really matter. Lifting my head causes my heart to freeze solid in my chest, my eyes connecting with Skeleton King's dark ones.

He reaches up, his long fingers combing through his warm brown hair just as Ingvar squeezes my hips. The thought of John's hands being on me instead of the ones that are, plants itself right in the front of my brain. I'm ashamed of myself for even thinking such a thing, but I bet he would be kind and gentle. I've never wanted someone to touch me this way before, but maybe he'd be different. There's a honey tint to his skin, and I wonder what it would look like next to my paleness.

His eyebrows narrow as his full lips press together, making me wonder what it must be like to kiss them. Suddenly, Ingvar's cock doesn't feel so bad.

Fink says Skeleton King only likes girls who have been buried. Still, the very idea of being with him has tingles spreading through my veins, shocking me when I rock backward. Even though I of course know it's Ingvar inside my body, with Skeleton King standing in front of me, it's easy to pretend it's him instead.

The spell is broken when Fink returns with money and a piece of paper, handing both to him.

"Would you like to stay for dinner? We'll be done here sh—"

"No." His response is so quick it even leaves Fink looking surprised. "I mean, thank you, I just have a busy night." Looking over his shoulder at me one last time, he frowns before leaving.

I've hardly ever spoken to him, so I can't imagine

what could be going on in his head, but with his face so fresh in my memory, he spends the rest of my punishment with me.

EXPERIMENTS
John Skelver

November 15ᵗʰ ~ Evening

I'D ALREADY BEEN STRUGGLING TO STOP THINKING of her after the Halloween Games, and in the two weeks since seeing her at Fink's, it's only gotten worse.

The night she held my hand in the graveyard, I went home to eliminate the arousal she doused me in. Natasha laid there waiting for me, yet when I touched her, the chilled stiffness of her skin didn't give me the comfort it normally did. My mind kept replaying the sensation of feeling Sarah's heat. The rush that consumed me at her touch. I still went through with it, emptying myself in Natasha's corpse, but the entire time it was with Sarah in mind. The images of her scarred, naked body are still very vivid as is the memory of her soft skin. Every time I was with Natasha, I came as I ran my fingers over her stitching, pretending they were Sarah's scars.

I even cut her face the way Sarah's is. I sigh as I look over to Natasha, whose stuffed body stands in the corner. She's getting used up; it'll be time to get rid of her soon.

I need a way to make the bodies *warm*. I have to believe that it will be enough. When Fink offered me Sarah, I was stunned, and part of me wanted so badly to say yes. I knew she wouldn't have been allowed to humiliate me by turning me away, though, I could never do that to her.

My breath is hot inside the mask as I open the jar of ethanol and pull out the small cut of skin that I removed from my most recent cadaver. It was a Jewish man this time, who I only dug up for research purposes. It goes against Jewish faith to embalm a body, and I needed a natural specimen. Heat does unpleasant things to dead flesh, so this is going to be a challenge, even with Fink and his equipment at my disposal. Fink basically told me at his house that this entire endeavor is a waste of my time and impossible, however it's not as if I have anything to lose by trying.

It was Fink who originally gave me the idea to taxidermize non-embalmed bodies so they'd last longer. I'll admit they don't look as pretty after they're skinned and reshaped over the molding. Regardless, they stay with me forever, which is more than I can say for any other woman. Every month or so, I get a new girl, and even though the embalmed ones are a lot less work, I don't have the same connection with them as I do the women I'm able to recreate with my own hands.

Lately, however, my focus has shifted past preservation to realism. If I can figure out a way to keep a corpse warm *and* preserved, it will be the closest I'll ever get to knowing what it feels like to be with a living woman.

It's a form of self-torment because even if Sarah wanted me, I don't know if I could physically do it. The idea terrifies me to my core. I don't know exactly when that fear started, but I do know the exact moment my life began heading toward this path.

Tears fall down my face in pain and frustration. I really liked Layla… a lot. I don't know what's wrong with me. What makes me so different? What is it about me that repels people? Specifically girls? I don't think I'm ugly, so I don't believe it's my looks. It's got to be deeper than that. I toss another rock in the lake with a groan.

She laughed at me. She mocked me in front of everyone, saying I was gross and pathetic. I had spent hours writing her that poem. I thought that if she could read in beautiful words what I felt about her, she would go to the freshman formal with me. I don't have any friends to talk to, and it sucks that I can't even go home and tell my mom. She always punishes me for the smallest mention of anything remotely sex related and that definitely includes girls. It's times like this when I feel guilty that part of me wishes my dad would have stayed. It would have been nice to have a guy to talk to.

I wipe the tears from my wet cheeks. Skipping another stone, it hits something on the second jump and falls flat into the river. My head tilts as I stand to my feet, curious. Reaching down, I grab a large stick to try to move whatever it is closer to me. When I realize I'm looking at human hair, my gaze travels down, forcing me to process that I'm seeing a body. My stomach freefalls, taking all the moisture in my mouth along for the ride. I use the stick to drag it up on the bank and then again to roll her over. Her face is pretty messed up, but her naked breasts are the first real ones I've ever seen. I look down between her open legs, and what's there gives me an instant hard-on. A real pussy.

Looking around to make sure I'm alone, I touch it. I suck in a sharp breath. She can't tell me I'm gross or pathetic. She can't reject me or make me feel perverted.

She can't hurt me at all. In fact, she can do the exact opposite…

While of course there were many other choices and factors that led to me becoming Skeleton King, the day I lost my virginity to a corpse changed my views on living women. I realized that they had never been an option for me. While I've never understood what makes me so different, so…wrong, the day on that river bank, I learned that I didn't need a breathing body, just *a* body. I could finally feel some version of affection without risking pain or cruelty. For either of us.

Placing the piece of flesh on a heat rock, I jump at the unexpected *ring* of the doorbell. After running up the stairs, I open the front door to the surprise of Sarah Stein hurrying down my walkway.

"Sarah?"

She stops mid step, her shoulders falling with her head before she slowly turns. "H-hi...um, I know you're working on some experiments, but I didn't know what type, so I just brought you some stuff that might help."

I look down, seeing a basket full of things like alkaline and arsenic. A smile tugs on my lips. That's really sweet.

"Thank you." I open the door farther and step to the side. "Would you like to come in for a drink? I promise I won't tell Fink."

She smiles then looks over her shoulder. "Um, yeah...sure."

Picking up the basket, I hold out my hand to invite her in. She follows me to my kitchen where I set her gift down on the counter before turning to the cupboard, removing two martini glasses. I'm not deluded enough to deny that I'm trying to impress her when I pull out the powdered dry ice to make the fanciest drink I know. After adding the ice to the glasses, I set to mixing brandy, grape juice, and vodka in a shaker.

She points to my hands. "Does that have alcohol? I'm not allowed liquor."

I grin without stopping what I'm doing because I can hear the interest in her question. I pour the mixture then add some grenadine. "It does…" Her eyebrows furrow as she watches me take out a bowl of strawberries for garnish. "I hope I've made it clear that I won't rat you out to Fink. Besides, how old are you, anyway? Aren't you a little curious?"

She holds up her fingers, obviously doing the math in her head. "Um…I'm eight—no, nineteen. And yeah, maybe a little…it's only, Fink says it will take away my self-control… make things blurry. I don't think I'd like that."

Nineteen…technically she's not old enough to drink, but I also have a stuffed corpse in my basement, so I can't say I'm a stickler for obeying

Mundane laws. Her eyes blaze, watching me add the last scoop of dry ice. "That's only if you have too much. Just try it, if you don't like it, then don't finish it."

Waiting for the ice to dissolve, I watch the white smoke float from the drinks, giving my dark kitchen an eerie feel. Hesitantly, she takes the cocktail from my hand, bringing it to her lips.

Her face twists up as she shudders. "This tastes weird..." she tries it again, "It's kinda good though."

"It's called 'Witch's Heart.'"

She snorts which is probably the most adorable sound I've ever heard. "Well that's dumb." I raise an eyebrow at her honesty and grin at her immediate backpedaling. "I—I mean, it's just, why would a witch's heart be purple? A witch is only a person that practices a certain religion, right? So—" her eyes widen as they meet mine. "Oh, God, you didn't name it did you? I'm sorry, it's not—"

I touch her arm to get her to relax, and I'm not sure if I regret it or revel in the feel of her again. My heartbeat quickens as I attempt to keep my voice steady. "I didn't name it, don't worry." I give her a smile, trying to coax one out of her. "Besides, you're not wrong. It is kind of dumb."

Her shoulders fall as the softest laugh releases from her lips. "Good."

Slowly taking my hand away from her skin normalizes my pulse while my eyes travel across the wounds on her face. They look like they might still be sore, although they're definitely healing. More than anything, I want to kiss over the scarring. Conjuring that image in my mind both disquiets and arouses me.

Sarah brings a hand up to her cheek. Her eyes are shimmery with what I worry are tears. "I know it's ugly. It's probably uncomfortable to look at."

She turns away from me which upsets me greatly. I'm not even sure why exactly. Unconsciously, I find myself touching her again. Her warmth does something to me, akin to a drug. Gently, I rub my thumb over the cuts, forcing myself not to press my lips to them. I can't. Touching her is already nearly too much.

I take her drink, placing it next to mine

on the counter as I nod to the basement door. "Follow me, I want to show you something."

The very second I say it, I wish I could take it back. I'd thought that maybe if she sees what I've done to Natasha, she'll know I don't find a single thing about her ugly. She knows what I do, so I'm not worried about scaring her, it's just that this has become a very personal thing. I'm about to share intimacy with a living woman, regardless of the fact that it isn't sexual.

Every step is harder to take than the last, and I become momentarily immobile when I feel her take my hand in her small one. Forcing one foot in front of the other, I lead her downstairs to my workroom.

She looks around with wide eyes at the taxidermy equipment and my various knickknacks. Her hand sets my skin ablaze, yet I squeeze tighter as I lead her to Natasha. I risk a glance at her to see her mouth in an *O*.

"This is Natasha. Well, her skin anyway."

"Her mouth…" The sound of her whimsical voice loosens every one of my tense muscles. She understands without my having to explain.

Turning to me, she gives me the most

beautiful smile, and in this moment, all I want to do is make sure it remains on her face. The sudden need to confess my true feelings about her situation chokes me, and yet, words seem insufficient. "You know…I've always hated the things Fink puts you through. I just…"

Her hand rests on my arm, lighting up every nerve in my body. "It's all I know, John. I honestly don't remember anything different." The torment in her eyes makes it clear that her nonchalance and casual tone are just a ruse. What I don't know is whether it's for her benefit or mine. "Besides, it's not as if there's anything you can do about it." Glancing next to us, she asks, "What's that?"

My eyes follow her gaze to my work table. "Shit!" Dropping her hand, I rush to the skin resting on the rock. I completely forgot about it. The flesh has started to cook, turning tough and dark. Damn it. I sigh and toss it into the container that I bring to Mammoth's morgue every month to burn in his crematorium.

"What is it you're doing exactly? I know that's why you came to Fink's the other day. You're trying to figure something out." I wish so badly that I was wearing my paint so I could hide behind Skeleton King. I'm too embarrassed to admit that she inspired my endeavor for heat. She quirks an eyebrow, and I frantically search my mind for words, any words just to form a sentence when she continues, "Why do you prefer dead girls?"

Each question that springs from her lips makes me more rigid. As the moisture on my tongue evaporates, my voice comes out scratchy and rough. "They're less…complicated." While it's a gross oversimplification, it's the best I can come up with in the moment.

Her eyes continue to roam my workshop as she fiddles with a loose thread on her dress. "Can I ask you something else?"

I'm terrified of what she will try to pry from me, yet I find myself nodding.

"Will you bring me down here? When I die, I mean?"

My skin flames as my stomach lurches into my throat. Recoiling back from her, I shake my head. How could she think that? I would never defile her in that way, never once have I even entertained the thought. I can't imagine destroying her beautiful body for my own perversions, and I hate that I made her fear that. "No! Of course not, Sarah."

Her eyes fall to the floor as she tenses. Crossing her arms, she murmurs, "Oh."

Instead of being relieved by my response, she seems hurt. I shake my head because this is exactly why I can't be with living women. They don't make any damn sense. "I could never desecrate you like that." I'm not speaking loudly, though, in the still silence of the room, it's heard as clear as glass.

Tilting her head, she scrunches her eyebrows, "John, I'm *asking* you to." Her arms fall to her sides as she holds out her hands. "I want you to…be with me."

The hammering of my heart makes me nauseous. I can feel my head shaking before I'm able to speak. The very idea is a source of nightmares.

"No," I say harsher than intended.

Just speaking of this makes me feel cut open and exposed. Vulnerable. Even with my fear of her saying that I repulse her, I ride the overwhelming ache to feel more of her. The lump in my throat rolls into my chest as I cup her neck at the base of her jaw. Her pulse thumps beneath my fingers, and I shudder while fighting every alarm bell in my brain. Softly tracing my thumb across her jaw, I lean forward, kissing her hard before I change my mind. The sensation of her lips moving against mine has me gasping into her mouth. Her fingers clench at my shirt, and when she presses her body against mine, her heat seeps through my clothes. Even as my aching, solid cock pushes against her stomach, she doesn't pull away.

Breaking our kiss, I whisper through heavy breathing, "I don't want you cold." She blinks a few times, stuttered puffs of air coming from her lips. I'd never noticed the pretty, light freckles sprinkled across her nose before. Panic constricts my chest as I finish my confession. "I want you just like this."

SPIDERWEBS
Sarah Stein

November 15th ~ Evening

IT FEELS LIKE BUGS ARE CRAWLING AROUND inside my stomach. John Skelver just kissed *me*. His words shuffle in my brain, trying to get organized so they make sense. Is he saying what I think he is? I raise my eyebrow, scared to hope so.

"Alive?"

His eyes keep falling to my mouth as his face twists into a tortured expression. I barely notice his subtle nod with how heavy he's breathing.

Once again, he crashes his mouth against mine, his hands squeezing my neck and waist. I've never experienced kissing like this before.

I'm certain that this is what it's meant to be. My veins crackle, and my heart feels like it's about to explode. When he pulls away from me, worry that he's thinking better of this makes my skin shrink against my bones.

"What's wrong?" I whisper

He looks behind him to the stairs. "I don't know if I can—" Shaking his head, he grabs my hand, squeezing my fingers so hard that they crush together. "Come on."

Urgency seems to overtake him as he runs up the steps, dragging me behind him. His shoes are loud on the floor as he pulls me through the main level to a spiral staircase. Nothing makes noises in his sleep when we pass him on the way to the top of the house.

Climbing off the final step, I gasp at the room in front of me. A large window makes up part of the curved wall, the lowering sun shining across all of Hallows Grove, giving an orange glow to the space and streaking across a massive, round bed sitting in the center.

"Wow. Is this your bedroom?"

I bite my lip as his fingers comb the hair from my face. His body is so close, his eyes searching for something in mine. "No. It's a place I come to think and occasionally to sleep. I've never been with any person, dead or alive in here." He deeply inhales before continuing, "Do you really want this? With me?" Stepping back, he keeps his hands on my arms. "Do I not disgust you?"

His question makes me terribly sad. It's crushing that he'd even think that. I softly touch my fingers over his mouth that I so desperately desire to kiss again. His dark eyes look so sad beneath his thick, long lashes. "I've wanted you for years, John. Not Skeleton King, not who everyone thinks you are. You."

I move my hand to his cheek where he leans in to my touch, his eyes closed tight. "I'm scared," he whispers.

"Why?"

After several long moments, his gaze finally meets mine. "Because you're breathing."

The confession stuns me. His decision to be with the dead stems from insecurity, not longing. Just as I open my mouth to tell him that he has nothing to be afraid of with me, my words are snuffed out by a kiss. His hands travel to my waist, lifting me up as I wrap my legs around him. I hold him firmly while he carries me to the bed, his lips constantly on my flesh. As he lays me down, his fingers slide up my thighs, giving me a rush I've never known. The anticipation is crippling. I can't grasp that I'm really here.

"This is okay, right?" The question comes out gravelly as his erection presses against my leg through his pants.

I reach up to smooth his scrunched brows. "This is perfect. Just keep going."

He fights to make eye contact, his voice wavering with uncertainty. "Will you tell me what you like? I...I honestly don't know."

His desperation for my approval makes arousal pool between my thighs. I reach for his hand, his breath hitching while my heart thrashes wildly at my ability to control this situation. He doesn't break his stare as I show him where I want his touch.

"This feels good," I tell him, pressing the pad of his pointer finger over my panties and moving it to rub my clit.

I thrust against his hand, showing him the tempo that I like. Taking a hold of his finger, I guide it beneath my panties.

He gasps, flinching once I push his thick digit inside. "Oh fuck, you're so warm," My stomach bubbles as he lowers his head, groaning against my chest. "So goddamn warm." The awe in his voice sends tingles all the way to my toes. Looking down reveals his cock straining in his jeans, so I release his hand to rub over the denim. As he continues moving his finger, his eyes explore my body. Rocking faster against his touch, I look up as the evening sun catches a spiderweb stretched across the corner of the ceiling. Its beauty is unexpected. Much like John's. "Shit." He stills above me. "This is intense, I don't know if I can…"

His jaw ticks beneath my palm when I gently touch his face. He's questioning this, and I can't let that happen. Reaching between us, I pop open the button on his pants and lower his zipper. The skin around his cock isn't loose like Ingvar's, allowing my thumb to rub over the raised flesh of his tip. My fingers are unable to reach fully around his shaft, meaning he's larger than Fink or Ingvar and it might be painful to have him inside me. Even if it is, it doesn't matter, all the pain in the world is worth him touching me. He throbs in my hand and as soon as I tighten my grip, his chest rises as if he's holding his breath. With a gentle touch, I stroke him, bringing my lips to his ear. "Please don't be afraid. This is all I've wanted for as long as I can remember."

He suddenly thrusts his hips, fucking my fist as he breathes out, "Okay." Lowering his gaze, he watches me pump him. "Jesus, Sarah…"

I'm the only girl in the whole world that has ever had the opportunity to show him how good someone living can make him feel, and I have every intention of taking advantage of that. "Will you lie on your back?"

His full lips lift into a smile as he climbs off of me. He tears the clothes from his body, revealing golden skin and the sharp lines that define his muscles. I snap my mouth shut once I realize it's fallen open from gaping at him. I've never seen someone so…solid. Grave digging is an effective work out, apparently.

Slowly lifting his eyes to mine, he rubs the back of his neck. I hate that he isn't more comfortable. I'm truly grateful that this is happening at all, I just also need him to know I mean what I say. "You're perfect to me. You always have been."

A grin that brightens his face and reveals his dimples tightens me to my core. While he's always been gorgeous, his smile makes him look ethereal.

His eagerness is back when he climbs on the bed, lying down like I asked. This is nothing like it is with Fink and Ingvar. I *want* this, and for once, I have the choice. The control. It's intoxicating.

Crawling between his legs, I grip him in my hand, spitting on his shaft to add lubrication. When I pick up my pace, he arches his back and fists the sheets. "No one has ever done this to me before…Oh, God."

His reaction to my touch is a heady feeling. And being his first living girl is an honor I can't even fully grasp. I know how paramount this is. I swear right now that I will make this an unforgettable experience for him. Then maybe, just maybe, he'll want to do it again.

He keeps his eyes closed as I wrap my mouth around his tip, taking him in slowly because my cheeks are still a little tender.

"What are you doing?!" I instantly stop, shifting my eyes up to him because I can't tell if he's angry. Did I cross a line? "Aren't you still healing?"

Continuing to jerk him, I smile at his concern. "I'm fine, Fink makes me do this all the time."

He glares at me. Shit. Was mentioning Fink bad?

"I'm going to talk to him—"

"NO!" I yell before covering my mouth at my outburst. "I'm sorry, but Fink *cannot* know about this." I keep my hand moving up and down his erection while I hate myself for bringing my captor into this. "Can we just not talk about him?"

The moment he nods, I take him back into my mouth, feeling his body tense beneath me. Eventually he relaxes as his hands tangle in my hair and grip my head. I'm touched by the obvious restraint he's using with his thrusts. He doesn't want to hurt me.

"Shit. Your mouth is so hot, I don't know how much longer I can last."

I need to feel him inside of me before I go home. I need this to fantasize about when I'm with Fink and Ingvar. Slowly sliding my mouth off of him, I kiss the tip before lifting my patchwork dress over my head. He stares at my chest before slowly reaching up to rub his thumb across my nipple. Soft moans stutter from my lips as his large hands fondle my breasts.

Since I'm still wearing my boots and socks, I try not to scratch him with the heel when I bring my leg across to straddle him. My heart beats so hard, it seems to echo around me.

Whoosh.

Whoosh.

Whoosh.

Whoosh.

His own chest rises and falls quickly as he watches me move my panties to the side. The idea of leaving them here as something for him to think of me by creates a tickle in my belly. Ripping each of the sides allows them to fall to his stomach. His eyes flip up to mine, and he opens his mouth to speak, yet instead, he just licks his lips when I toss them to the floor.

I thrust against the side of his erection,

lubricating him with my arousal. Shaking his head, his hands fly to my hips.

"Wait. What about a condom? Isn't that important for...you?"

He's stalling. He knows I've only been with Fink and Ingvar. For a split second, I question if I should keep going. What if he isn't sure he wants to do this? My body screams for me to take his cock inside it, to feel him the way nobody else with a pulse ever has, but my heart needs to know he truly wants this.

Moaning from the friction caused by rubbing myself against his length, I lean forward to press our mouths together. His instant response makes me giddy.

I cup his face and whisper, "I don't want to push you into anything. This is about both of us. Tell me to stop, and I'll stop."

He squeezes the back of my neck, pressing our foreheads together. "I swear, in this moment, I want this more than anything."

My smile is impossible to erase. He kisses me again before allowing me to sit up, watching intently as I slip the tip into my entrance. His head falls back while I take him deeper, his fingers clawing into my waist as I adjust to his size.

"Holy shit," he moans with his first few thrusts. A soft laugh releases from my lips, and he gives me an ornery smile. "This is fucking amazing."

It's as if he's suddenly allowed himself freedom when he begins pounding up into me so hard, I cry out.

Stopping abruptly, he lies immobile. "Fuck, I'm sorry. Did I hurt you?"

He's much more than his sinister reputation. His kindness is so pleasantly unexpected that I kiss him and shake my head. "I'll tell you if it hurts, I promise." Kissing down his neck, I grind my hips to feel him that deep again. I love the sensation of my breasts against his smooth chest. "Fuck me as hard as you want, John."

A squeal jumps from my mouth when he flips me onto my back so quickly it takes a moment to focus on him hovering above me. Muscles ripple in his large shoulders while he moves himself in and out of my body. He gently presses his lips over every inch of my flesh, making me realize he's kissing my scars.

All of them. Shocking waves shoot through my blood vessels as I clench around him, and I'm suddenly self-conscious about coming. I'm going to make a mess.

"Fucking fuck," he groans out. I squeeze his ass and widen my legs, pushing him deeper. "Should I pull out? I'm gonna come soon."

I shake my head, moaning out my answer. "No, I want you to do it inside me."

Though he wavers, tilting his head with a hesitant frown, he doesn't stop. As he continues to bring me closer, the barrier holding back my release thins with pressure, tightening my skin. I'm what Fink calls a 'squirter.' It's going to happen any second, and now, I wish I would have prepared him.

"John, I—" I'm too late when my flesh cracks apart. I whimper, thrusting as I feel myself gushing onto him, splattering against my stomach and legs.

I keep my eyes closed because I'm too embarrassed to look at his reaction until he shoves into me harder and faster.

"Oh, fuck, Sarah!"

I lift my eyelids, finding his stunning face

overtaken by pleasure. His body trembles when his warm seed spreads inside me. Even knowing I will never have a child, it's kind of fun to fantasize about having his. As he stills, his eyes meet mine, and for a split second, they look so kind. I think he's going to kiss me, when instead, he removes himself and pushes off the bed.

He tugs on his jeans, and when he looks at me again, his words are so sharp, they slice my heart right down the middle.

"You need to leave."

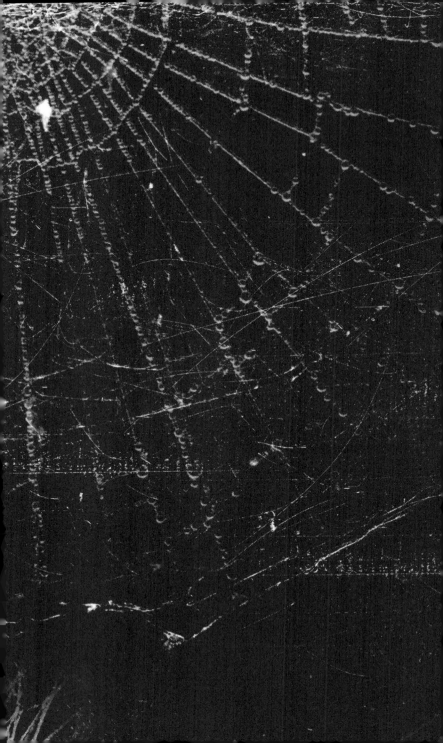

SELF-POLLUTION
John Skelver

November 15th ~ Evening

I'VE SEEN SOME HORRIFYING THINGS OVER THE years, but the look on her face sinks my stomach to the floor. She doesn't understand, I know that, yet my chest still feels as if it's being ripped apart from the pain I'm causing her. Although it may not be today or next week, eventually, she'll realize who I truly am. Inevitably, she'll turn me away someday. She'll be sickened by me. Ashamed she ever let me touch her. While losing this, what we had tonight, is already darkening my thoughts and bringing out my anger, the result would be significantly more horrendous if I lost her later.

I had a taste, and it's going to drive me mad.

I am Skeleton King. Gravedigger, taxidermist, and necrophiliac. The industry of decay is my kingdom, cemeteries my solace. I'm a nightmare merchant that thrives in the darkness. I belong in the cold, not with her light and warmth. Her beauty would only deteriorate in my presence.

"W—what?" She yanks her dress down over her head, covering her beautiful body in shame. I'm already shrouding her in my degeneration.

"I said to get the fuck out. Don't come back." I pull on my shirt and turn away from her. I can't bear to watch her tears fall.

I hear her shuffling off the bed, her boots *knocking* against the floor as she crosses the room. Her red hair covers her face when she hurries past me and down the stairs without looking back.

Rage at the fact that I had to do that boils up in my throat. It's as though my veins are turning black. "Fuck!" I grab a book sitting on a side table, throwing it across the room with a growl, breaking a few knickknacks in the process.

I remind myself that I made the right

decision. The torment would have sent me spiraling if I ever had to hear her say she didn't want me. Looking out the large window, I watch her running back to Fink's. Returning to more suffering at his hand. That's who we are as residents of Hallows Grove. Giving in to our deepest and darkest desires regardless of the effect on others.

My desperation to heat corpses is suddenly the only thing that matters. I will feel the warmth again without risking the humiliation of rejection.

I need a new body.

Nothing jumps up to follow me as I pass him, storming down to the basement. Carrying Natasha over to the steel table, I'm overwhelmed by the urgency to get rid of her. I grab a scalpel, cutting it crudely down her chest before peeling off the pieces of flesh. Once I remove the glass eyes, I place them in Barbicide and finish separating her skin from the mold. She's been my companion for weeks, yet now she's nothing more than a pile of old meat that I toss into a cardboard box. After throwing her clothes into the sanitization bucket to be washed, I drop the box of remains by the front door then go upstairs to shower.

Nothing watches me while I smoke a joint and paint the skull over my face. I don't even have to tell him to follow me when I'm finished. He's on my heels, ready for a ride in the car as I pick up the box containing what's left of Natasha.

The convenience of a town like Hallows Grove is that I have everything I could ever need at my disposal. Right now, it's the local mortician.

I drive the two streets over, telling Nothing to stay in my car before I carry the box to the back entrance and ring the bell. I always feel bad that I don't know the mortician's real name; everyone calls him Mammoth. The nickname is clearly a nod to his size because he's enormous. He's not the brightest crayon in the box, but he's always been nice to me. Although, I do feel bad for the animals he brings here, which is why I always make Nothing stay in the car.

He swings open the door, consuming the entire entryway in his overalls and yellow latex gloves.

"H—hello, John. M—more for the f—furnace?"

His stuttered voice is a deep baritone. I nod, letting him take the box, my eyes going to the large scar stretched across the left side of his bald head. From what I hear, he was stabbed with a butcher knife by his father when he was younger.

"Thanks, Mammoth. How are you enjoying the bunny? Is he still looking good?"

I taxidermized a rabbit he calls 'Easter' a few weeks ago. Regardless of the fact that the poor thing was in terribly rough shape when he gave it to me, I was pretty proud of it when I finished.

He nods and waves, which I'm assuming means it's the end of our conversation since this is how it seems to go every time. When he closes the door, I return to my car, heading to the library.

There's this new thing called 'internet' that serves as an ocean of information. I have an electronic mail address, I just haven't broken down and gotten a computer yet.

As I walk inside the library, I find Eunice

organizing returned books beneath the staircase. He gives me a goofy grin before turning his wheelchair to face me.

"Skeleton King!" The poor kid lost both legs a few years ago fucking around on the train tracks right outside of town. "Are you here for the computers?"

He already knows the answer, seeing as he starts leading me to the three machines lined up in the far corner. "Yeah, can I have an hour block?"

"Take as long as you want." As he logs me in, I look down at his greasy hair to see a spider crawling between the strands. I debate telling him when he says, "There you go, all set. Let me know if you need anything."

Scooting in the chair, I'm left to my devices. Nothing lies at my feet while I search all the obituaries I can find within a fifty-mile radius. I finally come across a young woman that was buried yesterday, about sixty miles from here, who died from an infection in her heart. From what I can tell, her family doesn't have any religious burial restrictions. The cemetery is much too far away for me to be finished by dawn, so I'll have to wait until tomorrow night.

Well damn it. That makes the time I spent putting on my skeleton face completely pointless.

Even thinking about going back home brings about flashes of Sarah's mouth on my skin, her body around mine, only confirming that I need this body as quickly as possible.

Although I am truly grateful to her for what she gave me, the memories she left behind will haunt me until the day I'm put into the ground.

November 16th ~ Night

SINCE I HADN'T HAD THE TIME TO SCOPE OUT THE cemetery's security, it was a twist of fate to find it small and unmonitored. Even if someone happened to see me, my face paint would eliminate any chance of identification.

Her name is Wendy. She's been embalmed, so I won't be able to taxidermize her, but right now, that's the least of my worries. With her bathed and naked in front of me, I'm not even slightly aroused. She lies across the steel table under heat lamps, wrapped in an electric blanket.

Even as I wait for her to warm up, there is no eagerness. I won't feel her hands caressing my skin or her mouth on my body. She won't voice her arousal or drench my cock with her come.

A quick lift of her top lip reveals that her mouth has been shut via needle injector. Using wire cutters, I snip the metal pieces from the pins in her gums. When her jaw falls open, I undo my pants and hold her head in place. Careful not to scrape my dick on her teeth, I push until I reach her throat.

It only takes a few pumps to know her mouth isn't going to help. She can't lick, suck, or moan around me. Frustrated, I give up, using a knife to give her Sarah's smile.

Once again, thinking of her makes the sick bubble in my gut as I picture what's currently happening to her just because she came to see me.

I'm not the least bit in the mood, but it's now

or never. Wendy's skin is already beginning to wrinkle, and I doubt I'll be able to do this twice. Closing my eyes, I allow my memories to carry me back to when Sarah was still here.

I've wanted you for years, John. Not Skeleton King, not who everyone thinks you are. You.

I'll never forget how soft she was, the way her hands felt on my back and stomach. My erection grows in my palm as I remember her red hair draping over her face while she pleasured me in a way I have never experienced.

Fuck me as hard as you want, John.

God, she was so willing it was invigorating. To be wanted like that is something I've always desired, and it was more fulfilling than I could have ever dreamed.

My fist pumps over my cock as I line the tip with Wendy's hole. Disappointment overtakes me when I realize the heat has only impacted her body on the outside. Inside she's still hard and cold.

Fuck. This isn't working. I pull out of her and resume stroking myself. I'm not that fond of masturbation. I can practically hear my mother's voice and see the shame on her face, making this feel dirty.

Whoa. This is what girls look like naked? My pajama pants lift up, and I'm getting that weird feeling again. The last time I touched it, it felt so good, it was just really scary. I thought I was dying when wet, sticky stuff shot out of my body. Not because it hurt, but because of the exact opposite. Nothing else I'd ever felt before came close to comparing to that.

Turning the page, I reach down, shuddering when my hand makes contact. The woman in the photo has a black, plastic penis inside of the hole between her legs. She looks like she really likes it too. The faster I move my hand the better it feels. Odd noises leave my lips, and when I don't think I can take anymore, it happens again. Even though my heart is beating so fast my chest hurts, I softly laugh at how incredible it is.

Dropping the magazine, I move to get cleaned up when my bedroom door flies open. She removed my lock for this exact reason. My face and body instantly burn up in shame and horror at the way she's looking at me.

"What vile things are you doing to yourself?!" she shrieks.

Her eyes flash to the open magazine before settling on the mess I've made, dripping down my leg. Repugnance and fury overtake her features as she lurches for the offensive material.

Attempting to cover myself, I apologize desperately. "Mom, I'm sorry, okay? I—"

Grabbing the back of my neck, she forces me, naked and dirty, into the hall.

"You will not self-rape in this house! This is why I never wanted a son. Most men in this world are immoral, disgusting, perverted animals. Just like you are, and just like your father was!"

I hate it when she compares me to him. The only thing I can think about when she mentions him is the last thing I ever saw him do.

While she rarely beats me, when she does it takes me days to recover. I have a feeling this is going to be one of those times. The moment I realize she's leading me to the back door, I shake my head. It's literally freezing out there.

"Please, Mom—"

"Get outside, and don't make me say it again."

With a shaky breath, I step onto the back porch where the frigid air blows across my bare skin. My teeth chatter as she steps out behind me. Considering

I'm nude, I'm thankful that our fence hides me from the neighbors. She bends down to turn on the hose as my heart pounds wildly in anticipation. Even as I pray that she's only trying to scare me, I know Mother's never been much for bluffing.

The moment the water touches my freezing skin, the sensation is scorching hot. It's so cold that it feels like it burns, making me scream from the agony of it. She sprays me enough to clean me off, and the second she drops the hose, I gasp and fall to my knees. Every muscle in my body screams in anguish.

Turning around, she opens the door to go inside. "I will not have a sexual deviant for a son." She gestures between my shaky legs. "With any luck, your sin snake will freeze right off. Twelve minutes, John."

She can't leave me out here. She's done some messed up things, but surely she's not that unhinged?

All hope drops to the snow when I watch her walk inside and hear the lock of the door.

Excruciating seconds pass, magnifying my fear that I'm actually going to die, naked in my backyard, before the twelve minutes are up.

Damn it. I hate that my mother can still

worm her way into my thoughts. Especially with my dick in my hand. I'm already getting soft again. This obviously isn't going to happen right now. Sighing, I zip up my pants before I turn off the lamps and take the heating blanket off of Wendy.

Maybe if I taxidermize a body that looks like Sarah? I could buy a wig, get a patchwork dress, and try to mimic her scars with stitching. It's too late to get another cadaver tonight, though, and I'm exhausted.

After a shower, I climb into bed where Nothing is already snoring. I close my eyes, falling asleep to thoughts of the only girl who's ever touched me.

SURPRISE

Sarah Stein

November 15th ~ Evening

THE TEARS REFUSE TO STOP AS I MAKE MY WAY back home. The idea of having to deal with Fink right now makes me sick. I just want to cry alone. Walking through downtown, I stop to sit next to the stone fence by the Old Town Hall. There's a patch of purple flowers, and I pick the petals off one by one. What did I do wrong? I know it was scary for him, but I tried to assure him as best I could.

I didn't think tonight could ever happen, so really, I should be thankful for the fact that John made my dreams come true at all. He completely changed, though, and so suddenly.

Fink's hurt me plenty of times, but it's never been this…deep. I feel so silly for believing that maybe we could… I don't know…be something. I'm honestly not sure what I expected.

I've been out for much too long. My punishment is going to be bad enough as it is. With a sigh, I drop the flowers in my hand, dusting the grass from my skirt when I stand up to go home.

Ogier Bognar's ominous black truck sits in front of my house when I arrive. I cross my fingers, hoping that he's keeping Fink too busy to notice my return.

Gently opening the door, I slink inside before tiptoeing across the entryway to my room.

"Welcome back, Sarah." Fink's voice coils its way down my spine as I slowly turn around.

He's standing upstairs next to Mr. Bognar, both men looking down over the mezzanine. Ingvar pouts at the base of the stairs, chewing on a dog biscuit. There's definitely something off.

I swallow because my mouth has suddenly gone dry. "Hi, Dad." I use the term I haven't called him in a long time, hoping it will soften him like it did in the past. "Hello, Mr. Bognar."

"Enough, Sarah!" Fink snaps. "You've never seen me as the father I've tried so hard to be. It's taken me ten years, but I finally realized that you won't ever be the person I want you to become. Tonight was the final straw in the scarecrow. The time has arrived for me to cut my losses and start over."

I shake my head. What does that mean? I have no idea where this is going, I just know it won't be pleasant.

Mr. Bognar makes his way down to meet me. "I've been waiting for this for a while. The triplets need a mother, and I would be honored if you would be my wife."

My heart turns to ice in my chest before sinking to my stomach. Ogier Bognar is a vicious man. I've heard what he does to the women he brings into his home. Being with him for one night is sure to be more terrifying than a lifetime with Fink. I don't think he's actually asking me, but on the off chance, I say, "That's a very kind offer, Mr. Bognar, I'm just not interested."

The smile on his face widens. "Are you going to get in the truck willingly, or should we start our fun now?"

While on a normal day, I would fight with everything I have to stop this, right now, I'm simply too tired. I try one last jab at Fink's emotions to maybe change his mind.

"If Fink doesn't love me anymore, then I don't care what you want from me."

I look to the man who has been my caretaker for more than half my life. The harsh coldness I'm met with slices me deeper than I could have ever expected. I always thought if he let me go, it would be freeing. I never dreamed it would ache like this.

Dropping my head, I follow Mr. Bognar outside. Neither Fink nor Ingvar tell me goodbye. I look one last time over my shoulder to see the front door already closed behind me.

As he leads me to his truck, he unlocks the doors and climbs into the driver seat. The moment I scoot myself into the passenger's side, he grins. "Why don't you give me a preview of what I just paid for. Lift your dress."

I suddenly wish I wouldn't have left my panties at John's. The moment I reveal my bare pussy lips, he groans. "Fuck, look at that pretty thing. Open your legs."

Biting back a sob, I do as he says. He spreads me apart with his fat, rough fingers before plunging one inside. After pumping a few times, he removes his hand to reveal John's come shiny on his skin. "You little whore," he laughs. "Where'd you get this from?"

Terror wraps around my throat as I choke, "It's Fink's."

Returning between my legs he jams his fingers back in hard. He doesn't respond, but his smirk suggests he doesn't believe me. "At least you aren't too worn out. Your cunt is still tight as fuck."

He doesn't stop his molestation until we pull up to his large home, and I suddenly realize that my cat, Vince, might not know where I went. Sadness envelopes me as I wonder if he'll think I abandoned him. Maybe if I do whatever I'm told for the next few weeks, Mr. Bognar will allow me to bring Vince here. He's all I have left.

I follow him inside, barely listening as he tells the triplets to go play so we can have time alone.

Even though it's a stupid thought because

he surely won't care, I wonder what John will think once he learns I'm Mr. Bognar's wife now.

With slingshots and a BB gun in hand, the Sanity Eaters run outside to cause trouble, leaving me alone with my new captor.

Turning on his heel, Mr. Bognar orders over his shoulder, "Go upstairs to the last door on the left. Take off your clothes and lie on the bed, legs spread. If you don't make this difficult, I might take it easy on you tonight."

"Of course, um... what do you want me to call you?"

He scoffs, "What do you think?" He waves me off as he makes his way down a hall. "My name, you dumb bitch. None of this 'Mr. Bognar' bullshit. Now quit stalling. I'll be up in a minute."

I nod, doing as he instructs. Lying on the bed, I let the tears fall. I can't believe I'm crying over Fink. As terrible as he is, a small part of me wanted so badly to believe him when he said that he loved me. Now I know it was never really true. I just wish he had at least let me have Vince and my music box.

With a sigh, I wipe away my tears. Ogier

will be in here soon, and it's always less painful if I'm aroused first. Reaching between my legs, I rub a finger over my clit before sliding it into my body, instantly feeling the slipperiness of John's come still inside me.

I'll never forget the way his voice sounded when he felt me for the first time, the way his entire body reacted every time I touched him. As I reminisce about the way he felt thrusting into me, I pump my fingers in and out.

I rarely make myself orgasm. My body gets used so much between Fink and Ingvar that I hardly ever have the desire. As my arousal builds, I suddenly question if this will somehow make Ogier angry. Since I'm wet enough for lubrication, I begrudgingly remove my fingers.

I lie here, open and waiting for a man that I have no desire for. Not that it matters. The only man I do want doesn't want me.

John was completely against the idea of keeping my corpse. When he told me why, it warmed me to my core, yet now all it does is break my heart. I had my chance with him, and now, it's over. I ruined it somehow. Regardless of his reason for being so cruel the last few minutes we were together, every other moment with him was bliss.

My thoughts of John take me away until the door swings open and Ogier walks into the room, wheeling in a cart that holds a torn burlap sack, a strange box with buttons, and some rope.

"Sit up."

The moment I do as he says, he throws the sack over my head, allowing it to fall to my waist before he adjusts it. There are holes strategically cut out for my mouth and breasts, making it fairly easy to breathe. Fastening the rope around my body, he removes my ability to use my arms. I can't see much besides his dark figure through the burlap fibers, but I can feel him tying the rope loosely around my neck which he immediately uses to yank me onto my back. His wet tongue laps at my exposed nipples, his thick beard scratchy against my skin. He suddenly bites down hard, making me cry out.

"You're going to need to be a lot tougher than that," he murmurs. I can sense his body shifting when he yanks on the rope again, pulling me up to where smooth skin meets my lips. "Fink said you're skilled with your mouth. Do a good job, and I'll keep the voltage low."

My skin beads with sweat wondering what exactly he means by that. Since I can't see or use my hands, I suck on anything that goes into my mouth. He tugs on the rope, his violent thrusts making me gag so horribly, I'm nervous I'll throw up on him.

"Fuck, it's been a while since I've been sucked this good. Keep it up, and we'll get along fine."

His weight disappears before a *zap*, *zap* sounds in my ear and the bed dips with his return. My pulse increases at the sensation of something squeezing tightly around my right nipple. Seconds later, the same happens to my left. Thin, what I think are wires, lay across my stomach while my clit is pinched in exactly the same way my nipples are.

"Did Fink ever electrocute you?"

My heart pounds against my ribs as tears instantly wet the material resting against my cheeks. "W-what? No." I shut my eyes in embarrassment at how pathetic my voice sounds, grateful that he can't see my face.

With a scoff, he responds in a dull tone. "Oh, fucking relax. It's no worse than the shock collars I use on the kids."

Fingers probe inside of me before he enters me with a hard thrust, making me gasp at the intrusion. I feel crushed by sorrow as it suddenly occurs to me that John is no longer the last person to be in my body.

Without adequate vision, I find myself pretending that it's him pounding into me instead of Ogier. My hips jerk, pushing against flesh as I remember how full John made me feel. I hear myself moan, thinking of the way the muscles in his arms rippled every time he thrusted his body into mine. My fantasies bring a tingle across my skin, prickling every nerve ending.

"Your lack of a womb gets my dick hard. The last thing I need is more fucking kids." His words jerk me from my imagination, and the moment I stop moving, a *zap* sends torturous needles stabbing through my clit and nipples. I scream as my body flails at the unexpected assault. "Goddamn, that feels amazing." His baritone laugh sends shivers across my skin despite my elevated body heat. I don't even register him using my hole anymore. My skin quakes with an unpleasant buzzing, and my most sensitive parts throb in pain. I'm so focused on how uncomfortable this is that I fail to participate, unable to give him the performance he expects.

Zap.

"Fuck!" I cry out from the excruciating currents running through me. I despise pain. That was one thing Fink was always somewhat conscientious of. Ogier obviously takes the opposite stance on the subject.

"I'm not going to let you just lay there. If you aren't going to make an effort, I'll make it for you." I nod beneath the burlap, rotating and rocking my hips with as much enthusiasm as I can muster. "Yeah, that's it. Like that. Fink was wrong, you are a fast learner. You simply need the right motivation." He pulls on the rope, his beard itching my face while he slides his fat tongue around in my mouth.

Luckily, I don't have to keep it up for much longer. I'm actually a little surprised at how quickly he moans out his release in my ear. The terrible little things squeezing all my tender places are removed, making me sigh as the cool air grants a small relief to the soreness.

"That wasn't bad for our first time." He sounds surprised as my arms are set free from their bindings and he unties the rope around my neck. The chilled air blowing from the vent above me kisses my face when he yanks the bag off my head. "Maybe next time I'll bring in a whore and see how well you eat pussy."

I feel guilty just thinking it, but the idea of having someone else to share the torment with is an exciting one. Regardless of what he makes us do to each other.

I blink, wiping the hair from my face as I sit up to watch him put, what I'm assuming is the electrocuting machine, up on a shelf in the closet. A ton of dials cover the square box and three wires with clamps attached to the ends are poking out of the side. While I worry that he'll use it every time, I'm more concerned about what else might be in store for me.

"You're free to move around the house as much as you want...until you make me regret it." He yanks up his pants and tugs on his shirt. "If you want to go outside, ask, and we'll see.

I'm not like Fink. I don't intend to hide you or keep you locked away, *but* the moment you disrespect or disobey me, you're in for a world of hurt, girl."

He shuts the door behind him as I fall back on the bed. Even though he said I don't have to stay in here, I oddly want to do just that. I'm feeling so many things right now that it's making my head hurt. Closing my eyes, I pull the blanket over my naked body. I'm just so tired.

November 16th ~ Afternoon

I'VE BEEN IN AND OUT OF SLEEP SINCE LAST NIGHT, only getting up to go to the bathroom or get a drink of water. I shift around as the door creaks open, revealing Ogier standing there with a girl close to my age. She has wavy blonde hair and a dog collar around her neck. "Get up," he barks.

I do as he says, standing in front of them as he orders the girl, "Take off her dress."

She walks up to me, and when her crystal

blue eyes connect with mine, there's a moment of silent conversation, as if she's apologizing. For what, I'm not sure. She's clearly not here on her own accord. "I'm Sarah," I tell her.

"Esty," she says. "My name's Esty."

"This isn't a goddamn social call. Your names don't matter. Now, both of you better get naked before you piss me off."

Without hesitation, her hands wrap around the hem of my dress. I lift my arms to make it easier for her to pull it over my head. She's wearing nothing more than a thin, white, silk dress with a lace hem. In one swift motion, she takes it off and drops it to the floor. I find myself becoming jealous of her flawless skin. Besides the dark red dots scattered across the insides of her elbows, she's free from scars.

"Esty, lie on the bed, and spread that bald pussy for Sarah."

"Yes, sir," she quickly responds, doing as he asks.

Going beyond his request, she begins fingering herself. It takes me a second to realize she isn't trying to be seductive. She's attempting to arouse herself, presumably so it's less painful.

"That's more like it, whore." Stepping over to me, Ogier grabs my hair to make me look at him. "Make her come, and I'll have a surprise for you tonight."

Any 'surprise' he has for me is sure to be unpleasant, but the alternative could be much worse. I crawl to the edge of the bed where her pink folds are held open. While I haven't ever done this myself, I've had it done to me plenty of times, so I know what I think feels good.

Sticking my tongue out, I lick at the bump that swells above her entrance. I slide a finger into her hole, and the faster I lick her, the more she grinds against my mouth. I'm not necessarily turned on, but I like that she's enjoying herself. Based on the little amount of interaction I've had with her, she seems nice.

Ogier groans behind me as he pushes my head down, smothering me with her pussy. She apparently likes the sensation because her arousal seeps into my mouth and nostrils as she comes.

"That's a good girl, Sarah. Eat her fucking cunt." His body heat presses against my rear and thighs before he wipes his cock over my pussy lips and shoves inside of me. I cry against her wetness at the unexpected stretching of my body.

It only lasts a few minutes before he tells me, "Sit on her face."

As he pulls out, I adjust myself to straddle over her mouth. He lowers himself between her legs, immediately thrusting into her. I'm surprised at how pleasant her hot breath feels, blowing against my clit as she moans in response to his body moving inside hers.

Ogier pulls my hair, bringing me face to face with his assault on her cunt. After pumping inside of her a few times, he pulls out to force himself down my throat.

The entire time, her tongue laps at me with expert pressure, and it feels so damn good that I pathetically ride her mouth to reach my climax. I switch between licking at her little pink clit and Ogier's shaft as he slides in and out of Esty's body.

"Fuck," he groans. "I'm gonna come soon. Who wants it?"

I have the sense that eagerness can be rewarded, and she must've arrived at the same conclusion since we both say at the same time, "I do."

He laughs as he pulls out of Esty. "Too bad I can't keep you both." Walking over to the closet, he reaches up, though, I can't tell what it is he retrieves. "Kiss each other."

Esty's straddles me, her lips immediately finding mine as she lays me back on the bed. I can feel her wet pussy rubbing against my stomach while her tongue tastes my mouth.

Ogier groans, "I think I might actually feel a little sorry about this." He thrusts into her body, making her rock on top on me. Suddenly, her body shoves hard against mine when something hot and wet splashes over my chest. She coughs, splattering the dark liquid across my face. My eyes take a moment to focus, and when I can see clearly, there's a gaping red cut stretched across Esty's throat. She gurgles her last breaths while Ogier's fingers dig into the wound. He moans his pleasure, emptying himself into her dying body as he fingers the gash in her neck.

My eyes meet with Esty's, and I scream at the horror I see in them. *I'm sorry*, I mouth to her, hoping she knows that I truly am. None of this is fair, for either of us. Hot tears pour from my eyes with the last few gurgling sounds that escape her lips until her lifeless body falls limp and bloody against mine.

Slowly sliding out of her corpse, Ogier smiles at me, licking the blood from his fingers. "She was pretty great, wasn't she?"

"Why did you kill her?!" I scream at him. "She didn't do anything wrong!" She could have maybe been my friend...

I'm so angry at these men for thinking they deserve to have power over our bodies and lives. He lifts her off of me and tosses her corpse on the floor.

His nose is nearly touching mine when he says in a low voice, "I don't owe you shit, especially not an explanation, so I'm only saying this one time. She has more than one use, and so will you if you ever speak to me like that again."

All I want to do is spit in his face, but I turn my head to look at Esty's hollow expression, crying when he picks her up and carries her out of the room.

Curling into a ball on the bed, I allow myself to let go of the tears. I've never known anyone who died before. Even though I only knew her for a few minutes and we barely spoke, this hurts so badly.

He said she has more than one use, so I wonder if he's giving her to John. For so many reasons, I hate the thought of him touching her body.

Ogier doesn't come back for hours. The moon has been in the sky for a while, and I haven't moved from the position he left me in.

The pillow is soaking wet against my face when he snaps, "Get your ass out of bed, and come help me with dinner."

Standing in the doorway, his face reads impatience, so I murmur, "All right, Ogier."

I throw on my dress, and once my shoes and socks are back on, I make my way to the kitchen where he's checking on the food in the oven. He doesn't look at me when he points to a cutting board on the counter. "Start making a salad."

I'm grateful for the silence until shouting and yelling booms down the hall as the triplets bang their way through the house.

Jolt glares at me as she wraps her arms around Ogier to hug him. "What is?"

Bolt sits, stabbing his knife into the wood of the kitchen table. "She still?"

"Doing here?" Cask finishes while lifting up the back of my dress.

I spin around in surprise when Ogier laughs. "Cask, stop trying to look up your mother's skirt." They all stop mid-movement, gaping at their father. "That's why she's here. She's my new wife."

"We're not."

"Calling her."

"Mommy." The triplets piece out their reply.

He rolls his eyes, lighting a cigar as he opens the refrigerator for a beer. "Call her whatever the fuck you want, just get used to her because I paid good money for that tight little pussy, and she's not going anywhere."

Jolt takes her seat at the table, grinning at Bolt before looking to me. "Hey, rag doll?"

"Wanna play?" Bolt smirks at me in an unnerving way.

"A game?" Cask concludes.

I've never trusted the Sanity Eaters, and up until now I've been able to avoid them. Looking at Ogier tells me nothing about how he prefers I respond to this. I'm not dumb enough to believe this game will be the fun kind, but maybe if I play with them, I can get on their good side and they'll leave me alone.

Picking up the plates and silverware, I carry them to the table. "Um…okay. What's it called?"

"Just."

"Don't."

"Flinch."

The name of the game is equally as comforting as the unsettling smiles all three are giving me. Swallowing, I take my seat next to Jolt. She holds my hand, laying it flat on the table before spreading my fingers far apart. Both boys are watching her intently as Ogier remains silent by the counter.

"Remember," Jolt says. "Just."

"Don't."

"Flinch."

She pulls out the knife protruding from the table before slamming it in between my pointer and middle finger. Faster and faster she stabs it between my spread fingers as her and her brothers take turns singing a nursery rhyme.

"Early in the morning and the middle of the night."

"Two dead boys got up to fight."

"Back to back."

"They faced each other."

"Drew their swords."

"And shot each other."

On the last word, the blade slices the side of my ring finger and I gasp, pulling back my hand as they laugh.

"All right, that's enough," Ogier chuckles. "I prefer her to have use of her fingers." Reaching down for my cut hand, he rubs it over the growing erection in his pants, smearing the blood and winking at me when I make eye contact.

After what he did this afternoon, I can barely stand to touch him. Even though the triplets don't seem fazed, it makes me uncomfortable that he's doing this in front of the kids.

"Mmm," he groans. "Why don't you use that mouth to hold me over until after dinner?" Lowering his zipper, his hand immediately pushes my head down, forcing himself between my lips.

I hate that the kids are here, watching this, and I just pray that this is as far as it goes. He squeezes my ears, forcing me to gag every time he pounds himself all the way to the base.

Finally, he releases me, fastening his pants as I gasp for air. "We'll continue this after dinner. Go finish the salad."

I sigh in relief, grateful to do something normal like making supper. Adding the tomato wedges, I reach for the dressing.

Knock, knock, knock, knock.

Knock, knock, knock, knock.

My shoulders hunch as I jump at the loud noise. Spinning around, I see the triplets slamming their forks and knives against the table.

"We."

"Want."

"Food!"

"We."

"Want."

"Food!"

Ogier pulls out a roast with vegetables,

shaking his head in irritation. "Shut up, you little pricks. Don't make me get the dog collars."

I hand bowls of salad to the kids while Ogier places the roast in the center of the table. We take our seats while he fills each of our plates. The kids aren't touching their food, so I don't either. It isn't until Ogier sits and takes his first bite that the triplets dig in like feral animals.

While I swallow a bite of salad, Ogier points his fork at me. "Try the meat."

He watches intently as I pick up the knife, not taking his eyes off me until I cut a piece and place it in my mouth. This must appease him because he stops watching me to go back to his own food.

For once, the triplets' mouths are too full to make a bunch of noise, allowing us to all eat in peace. The piece of roast I bite off is really big, getting caught in my throat. I'm taking a sip to swallow it down when Ogier asks, "So? Does she taste as good as she did earlier?" I shake my head, unsure of what he means. He points to my plate, "Esty."

When the gears in my mind click in place, I drop my fork, instantly gagging at the knowledge of what I just consumed. That was her other 'use.' Falling out of my chair to the floor, I choke until chunks of barely digested meat land on the linoleum.

"Ewe!"

"That's."

"Nasty!"

Ogier's chair rumbles against the floorboards before the stabbing pain of him yanking me up by my hair shoots down my neck. "Fink was right about one thing: you're an ungrateful cunt!" He spits his words in my face. Reaching back, he brings his palm against my cheek so hard, I fall face down into my vomit. "Clean this up then go to your fucking room. I better not see you again tonight."

I fight hard to hold back my tears while wiping up the puke and cleaning the floor. None of them speak to me again, and I appreciate that.

My dress is soiled, but I don't dare ask if I can clean it, so I just wear it to bed. My stomach turns every time I think about what I've just done.

And he'll probably make me do it again and again.

There are things I could tell myself that would help me endure this new life. If I learned anything from being raised by Fink, it's that accepting and adapting to a situation is the only way to survive it. I just don't know if I want to anymore.

REPLACING SARAH
John Skelver

November 17th ~ Morning

I DON'T EVEN BOTHER TO SMOKE A JOINT OR DRINK a cup of coffee before jumping in my car to drive into the Mundane World. While Hallows Grove has many resources, we don't have much in the way of common consumerism.

There's a thrift store fairly close by where I can find things to make her dress. I won't be able to buy the same one Sarah wears because she made it. When she was younger, Fink would only get her new clothes when she grew out of them. He eventually taught her to sew, and as she got bigger, she began combining the fabric together to make the dress she now wears, adding to it whenever she needs.

Once I reach the store, I look for designs that I think Sarah would like. I'm immediately drawn to the clothes with floral print because she always seems to be picking flowers when she's outside. I choose a red, swirly skirt that's close to the same shade of her hair, striped pajama pants that are reminiscent of the socks she always wears, and a T-shirt that reminds me of her scars. With more than enough to recreate her dress, I make my purchase, asking the sales clerk for a phone book to search for the closest wig shop.

Though I find one nearby, it's a big disappointment. Aside from a short one of similar color, there's nothing comparable to Sarah's hair. Just as I'm about to leave, a flash of red catches my eye. Under a bunch of discounted wigs, I find it. It's perfect. Long, exactly like hers, and the perfect bright shade.

Excitement sends my nerves into a frenzy. I take a few breaths, telling myself I can't rush finding a body. It has to be exact, fresh, and naturally buried, so it may take time. As I sit in my car looking at my purchases, I conjure every detail of Sarah that I can from memory.

Her eyes. I'll need new ones that are her dark shade of hunter green. Her pupils are abnormally small, though, so I doubt I'll find exact matches. I'll also need to make a new mold especially for her.

The urge to get started has me speeding home. Everything will need to be ready for when I find my perfect Sarah. As soon as I walk into my house, I take my shopping bags downstairs, repulsed at Wendy still lying on the table.

Her embalming makes her insides useless to me, and since I don't have any current skin orders to fill, I'll need Mammoth to help get rid of her.

As I call him to ask that he pick her up, Nothing keeps chewing on the phone cord, making me sound insane from snapping, "Stop that," after every three words.

Mammoth tells me he'll be here within the hour, so I toss Wendy's cadaver over my shoulder, carrying her out back to drop her on the bottom step.

Time whirs around me as I clean and get organized, all my thoughts focused on preparing for my newest project.

Nothing whines behind me until I look at him. "What, buddy?" My jaw drops when I see he's holding Sarah's torn, pink, striped panties in his mouth. I laugh in disbelief. "Maybe you really do understand." Leaning down to take them, I scratch behind his ears. "That's a good boy, Nothing."

She was obviously so upset that she forgot them, which gives me a strange mix of sadness and arousal. I bring them to my nose, inhaling deeply when I find that her scent is still present, assaulting my mind with memories. I can almost taste her breath and feel her pulse. I've never experienced anything so fucking.... blissful. Even though my erection almost hurts, I lay the undergarment on the table and continue with my plans.

After combing the wig, I make a list of what else I need and sketch out a rough idea of how my Sarah will look. Finding as many blank papers and colored pencils as I can find, I draw my fantasies. Once I have a blueprint of Sarah that I'm pleased with, I pull out the clothes I chose from the thrift shop and place them next to her panties. I'll need a pattern, seeing as I really have no idea how to make a dress.

Running upstairs, I grab my keys when there's a loud *knock* at my front door. I look at my watch which tells me it's late into the day and not an unrealistic time for visitors. As soon as I answer, I roll my eyes at the Sanity Eaters standing on my doorstep.

"What do you guys want? I'm busy."

Jolt holds up a black trash bag and grumbles, "Daddy told us."

"To bring you what," Cask pouts in between the massive licks he's taking off his lollipop.

Bolt drops his own bag on the porch with excessive force. "We couldn't use."

Ogier always does this. Whenever he's finished with a body, he gives me his leftovers so he doesn't have to go through the hassle of getting rid of them. Picking up the bags, I drop them inside the door. All three of the triplets are frowning, in a worse mood than normal.

"What crawled up your asses?"

Bolt crosses his arms and nods toward their house. "We hate."

Cask assaults his candy in between his

words. "That stupid."

"Rag doll," Jolt sneers.

Wait…Rag doll?

"Sarah is at your house? Why?" My thoughts trip over themselves, trying to make sense of this. Did something happen to Fink?

"She is."

"Our new."

"Mommy."

It always takes a second to process what they're saying because of the annoying as fuck way they talk, but once I do, fire burns up my spine, erupting from my throat as I bellow, "WHAT?!" I'm suddenly split between rage and my fear for Sarah and Fink. I know what Ogier does to his whores, so I can only imagine Sarah's fate won't be any less brutal. "What did that motherfucker do to Fink?" They all look at each other, shoulders shrugging, clearly clueless. I scoff as I nod down my driveway. "All right, get out of here."

There's no way Fink would ever willingly let Sarah go. If Ogier took her from him, then he's undoubtedly out of control.

Rushing to the linen closet, I take the black

box off the top shelf and remove the lid. I bought this thing years ago and have never once used it. Opening the chamber, I slide in the six bullets before I point a finger at Nothing. "Stay home, boy."

My mind creates images of the possible circumstances I might find her in. I can't come up with a single positive explanation for why she'd be at the Bognar house. As terrible as Fink is to her, I truly believe he cares for her. But Ogier is under no such delusion. He'll destroy her.

I'm not thinking this through, which is unlike me, however, when it comes to Sarah, I have a tendency to react differently than I normally would. I'm done being a spectator while yet another man in this town rips her apart.

Once I arrive at the Bognar's driveway, I slow my steps. I have no idea what I'll be walking in on. I really don't want to see him doing something horrific to her.

Knocking seems stupid, so I simply walk in through the front door. The scene before me is the last I expected, stopping me dead in my tracks.

Fink is absolutely fine. More than fine by the looks of it. He sits next to Ogier, holding a glass in his hand, laughing at whatever had been said before I arrived.

They both look at me with bewildered expressions. "John?" Fink turns to me, leaning on his cane. "What's wrong, my boy?"

This doesn't make any sense. What the hell is going on? "Where's Sarah?"

Ogier raises his brows, taking a sip of his drink. "No disrespect, Skeleton King, but that's none of your goddamn business."

I jerk my head to Fink. "Did you...Did you just *give* her to him?!"

He answers me with a subtle nod that skyrockets my body heat. What was it all for? Why do everything he did to her, just to toss her away? I don't think I've ever been so fucking enraged with anyone in my life.

With a snort, Ogier stands, gesturing to Fink. "Hardly. I paid this asshole a nice chunk of change for that pussy."

Hearing him talk about Sarah like she's one of his whores blows the lid off the rage that's been boiling in my gut since the triplets came over. Before my brain can catch up, my fist is slamming into his face with more force than I even knew I possessed. The hit catches him off guard, making him stumble. There's nothing within his reach for him to hold on to, so he falls hard on his back.

I'm not stupid enough to believe I have a chance against him in a fist fight, so I take advantage of the situation by jumping on his stomach as I pull the handgun from my jeans, holding it to his head.

"Where is she?"

The hardness of my voice makes it unrecognizable to my own ears. Even if he tells me, then what? Am I actually going to shoot him to get her out of here? I've never killed anyone before. What will happen to me after this? I've broken a handful of our laws already.

When Ogier pushes his head harder against the barrel and smiles at me in his hideous way, I know there's no way this will end with both of us alive.

BATH TUB
Sarah Stein

November 17th ~ Midday

"**R**AG DOLL!" SOMETHING KEEPS STRIKING me on my thigh, forcing my eyes to pop open. "Wake up!"

The window shows the setting sun, meaning I've been sleeping for an entire day. Jolt keeps hitting my leg with her BB gun, so I sit up and grab the barrel. "Stop that. What do you want?"

"Daddy says," Bolt crosses his arms.

"You need." Cask jumps next to me on the bed.

"To come downstairs." Jolt rips the gun from my grasp.

I'm still groggy from sleep as I try to follow

what they're saying. "Why?"

"Because he," Bolt snaps as he opens my door.

"Said so," Cask adds.

Jolt attempts to drag me out of bed while yelling at me, "You dumb rag doll!"

As soon as I'm in the hall, I hear Fink's unmistakable chuckle. "I shouldn't laugh, but I can imagine that was quite the surprise for her." My skin feels itchy just knowing he's so close. I had hoped I'd have more time before having to see him again.

I follow the Sanity Eaters downstairs into the main living room where Ogier is standing next to Fink, Ingvar and a little girl I've never seen before. It takes a moment for me to deduce why she's here. When I do, I can't breathe. This is what Fink meant about starting over.

No...

He's already replaced me. She looks just like I do. It's hard to breathe when she looks up at me with sad, wide eyes. "Sarah, go get us something to eat." Ogier orders. I can't make myself look at Fink or Ingvar, but it's difficult taking my eyes off the little girl. "Now!" he barks.

Nearly tripping over my own feet, I hurry toward the kitchen to arrange a vegetable and fruit plate. I strain my ears to hear what they're saying, but the Sanity Eaters bang their way down the hall, making it impossible. They pass me on their way to the basement, not even acknowledging me when I ask if they want something to eat.

Before I'm finished arranging the plate, all three of them run back through the kitchen with large trash bags in their hands.

While I return to the living room, I hear Ogier's deep voice playfully saying. "I'd be glad to give you a demonstration."

I keep my eyes on the floor, even though they fight to look at the little girl again. It feels like it's all my fault that she's here...with him.

Setting the plate on the table, I can sense Fink's eyes on me. "I might take you up on that. You're free to one as well, you know."

Ogier's laugh is loud in my ear as he pulls me onto his lap, lifting my dress before his fingers intrude my body. "My great grandfather was into the kiddie thing, but it's not really my flavor."

His erection hardens beneath my butt, my thoughts getting tangled with the possibilities of what he'll make me do next when he smacks my pussy and pushes me off of him. I'm able to stop myself from falling when he says, "Go through Jolt's clothes in the basement and bring up what you think will fit this little one." His hand waves in the girl's direction.

Nodding my obedience, I make my way downstairs to do as he asks. Plastic tubs sit stacked in the corner, and I'm grateful that Ogier had the organizational foresight to label them. After pulling off the top four boxes from the first stack, I finally find one labeled: *Jolt size 8-10*.

I find myself searching for dresses until I realize I'm doing it because I know Fink prefers them. Settling on the cold floor, I begin separating the clothing into size and style. Just as I'm enjoying the peace and quiet, a loud *bang* startles me so badly I jump. As I turn my head to look up the stairs, I see the triplets dragging the little girl, whose eyes are large with terror.

"What are you guys doing?"

"Dad told us." Bolt tugs on one of her arms, attempting to force her down the steps.

Running to the bench, Jolt picks up an extension cord. "To play with her."

"Mind your." Cask frowns as he passes me on his way to the baseball bat rack hanging from the wall.

"Own business, Rag doll." Jolt huffs, turning to help Bolt get the little girl into the old clawfoot bathtub.

I'm proud of the child as I watch her use all her strength to make shoving her inside of the tub as difficult as possible for Bolt and Jolt.

"Would you guys leave her alone? Can't you tell she's scared?"

Jolt holds out the extension cord, her brothers taking hold of it to run in a circle and bind the girl with it. "You better shut up." Bolt snaps.

Picking up a dirty rag off the floor, Jolt says, "Or we'll tell Daddy."

"You're being mean." Cask hands a bat to Bolt as Jolt ties the soiled rag around the girl's face to cover her eyes.

She's sniffling now, and while I wish

they wouldn't involve her, I know they won't actually harm her. Not like Fink does. Climbing inside the tub with her, all three of them hit their bats against the edge, making her scream. They swing the bats right by her face, though, they don't ever actually touch her while they sing.

"Stay still."

"Is what we said."

"Move and we'll beat in your head."

The little girl sobs, and I sigh. "They won't really hurt you. Just play along, okay?" She doesn't answer, but her crying stops as the triplets keep singing.

An odd sound comes from upstairs. I can't place what it is, so I hold up my hand to quiet them, which they of course ignore. Tilting my head to listen closer, I slowly climb up the steps. As soon as I open the door to the basement it's clear someone is yelling.

With the triplets busy torturing the terrified child, I lock the door and sneak to the kitchen. Fink's voice freezes my shoes to the linoleum when he yells, "John! Stop!"

My feet move before my brain can intervene, carrying me down the hall to the living room.

Every wisp of breath escapes my lungs when I see John straddling Ogier while pressing a gun against his temple and screaming in his face.

"Where is she?!" His voice echoes off the walls as his body shakes on top of Ogier's. Is he...here for me? I shake my head because that's such a ridiculous notion.

"Ingvar, stop him!" Fink orders, gesturing toward John.

"No!" Ogier demands. "I want to see what this little cunt is made of."

Fink calls off Ingvar as John digs the gun deeper into Ogier's temple. His voice takes on a frantic tone. "The next time I ask it will be with a bullet in your brain." John's fury is something I've rarely seen over the years and never, ever to this extreme. It's mesmerizing.

Ogier's laugh suggests he isn't affected by John's threat in the least. "You're too pathetic to pull that trigger." When John doesn't respond, Ogier grins. "Get off of me, you fucking pussy."

John's shoulders tense, and I'm scared if I don't speak, he'll actually shoot him. Killing a Hallows Grove resident, especially one as prominent as Ogier, is strictly forbidden. "Stop!"

John whips his head around, his eyes widening at the sight of me.

Time freezes me in place, refusing to grant me the ability to move. We stare at each other for what feels like an eternity when he suddenly lurches to his feet, rushing across the room to stand in front of me.

A slow breath escapes from his lips as he reaches up to move the hair from my face. "Are you…are you okay?"

His expression is pained as he jerks his touch away from me. Despite how kind he's being in this moment, my mind replays the memories of the last time we were together. How he made me feel more alive than I ever have before only to hurt me deeper than Fink ever did.

"Do you really care?"

His eyes close with his sigh. "Sarah—"

"What's your plan here, Skeleton King?" A red faced Ogier growls. "It's well within my right to have her. I purchased her fair and square. Now… if you want to make a deal, we can discuss it, but I highly doubt that your pockets are deep enough."

John's jaw ticks as my eyes lock on the

vein bulging in his neck. "She's not one of your fucking whores! She's Sarah, for God's sake!"

"And that's why I wanted her as my bride. She's beautiful, young, and infertile." John's eyebrows furrow before he looks down at me. He didn't know. I always assumed he was aware of my inability to have children. "Absolute perfection." Even with John's hair in his eyes, I can tell they are full of sorrow, I'm just not sure if it's from pity or disappointment.

Keeping the gun on Ogier, he whispers, "I know you're angry with me, but please, just go back to my house, okay?" I open my mouth to protest. I want to stay and see what's going to happen, yet when he reaches out to place his hand on my cheek, all my oxygen is stolen, making it impossible to verbally protest. "I'm so sorry." The sincerity in his voice and the pain on his face wrings all the blood from my heart. I nod to him when he tilts his head toward the door, turning all of his attention back to the men in the room. "Wait for me. I'll meet you there soon."

Stealing a glance at Fink who is staring at me as if he wishes I were dead, I swallow and push past the fear of him I think I will always have and whisper, "There's a little girl downstairs with the triplets. Please help her, John."

He tilts his head in confusion when something crosses his face that I can only hope is him making the connection that I need him to.

When he nods his head, I obey his wishes and walk out Ogier's front door, truly free for the first time I can remember.

REVELATION
John Skelver

November 17th ~Midday

I WAIT UNTIL SHE'S SAFE AND THE DOOR IS SHUT before I close in on Fink. Shaking my head, I attempt to steady my hands. "After everything you've done to her, you just toss her away like an old sweater?!" My fist clenches around the gun with every step I take closer to him. "I've sat by and watched you take her apart bit by bit for years, seen her eyes lose the sparkle they used to have, so I'm not blameless either, but fuck, Fink! I always thought you loved her..." Ogier moves toward me, and I point the handgun at him. "Don't fucking move."

Fink leans against his cane with narrowed

eyes, holding up a hand to calm me. "I'm not a fan of the tone, Skeleton King. She was mine to do with what I wished. Not that I need to explain myself, but she became insubordinate and more trouble than she was worth. And I did love her. That's why I kept her for as long as I did." Tilting his head, he takes a step toward me. "You're walking on dangerous ground, John."

He's right. If I'm lucky, I'll be banished. If not, I'll end up as one of the Skeletons hanging from the tree downtown. Honestly, I don't care anymore. If it means Sarah is safe and free, they can do whatever they want to me.

"Maybe, but I swear to God, none of you will ever hurt her again."

Fink drops his head with a sigh. "If that's how you want to play this, John." He nods to Ingvar who barrels toward me so fast, I'm not able to prepare myself before he knocks me backward.

BANG!

The gun goes off in my hand before I drop it and my head slams on the floor. I hear a loud *thud* as my fist lands against Ingvar's jaw, which does literally nothing. He stares down at me with his dumb grin before punching me in the gut. The air is cut off from my lungs as I groan, wishing I could roll over. Without hesitation, he hits me in the face so hard, my head snaps to the side.

"Ogier!" Fink yells from behind me, though, I'm too busy getting my ass kicked to see why. Ingvar is hitting blindly, and my vision can't absorb anything past his swinging limbs. I take the dirty way out and jab my finger in his eye, giving me the break in his assault that I need. I slam my knee against his dick, which I know has been inside of Sarah, making him roll on his back, wailing in pain. As soon as he grabs his groin, I jump on top of him, grabbing his lopsided ears to bang his head against the wooden floor.

The nightmare they put her through and the horrors I looked past weigh heavy on my shoulders and rip through my veins. Over and over, harder and harder. In the back of my mind, I register that Fink is speaking into the phone, but all I can hear is my own voice with every crash of Ingvar's head against the floor.

"Fuck you, you fucking fuck!"

It isn't until I realize he's completely stopped moving that I release him. My breath is loud in my ears as I look down at the blood seeping from his skull. His eyes remain closed, though the subtle rising of his chest tells me he's still alive. Panting, I climb off him, picking up my gun on my way to Fink who's sitting next to Ogier's unmoving body. I'm not sure if it's adrenaline or if I truly don't care that I may have just killed him.

"You will pay dearly for this, John," Fink says through grinding teeth.

It feels like I never truly knew him. Or maybe it's myself I've never really known. I point the gun at his head as I back away toward the basement. "Follow me, and I'll put a bullet in your demented brain." Without Ingvar conscious, he doesn't have his muscle to stop me.

I don't turn my back on him until I reach the kitchen. I know where the basement is because years ago, Ogier went through a meth cooking stint. He made it in a bathtub down there until he decided meth heads weren't the most reliable businessmen.

The door leading downstairs is locked, so I turn the thin metal piece to release the catch. The triplets are lined up in a row on the landing. Bolt gasps the moment he sees me. "Skeleton King!"

It breaks my heart to watch their faces light up one by one.

"What's going on?" Cask asks with a furrowed brow.

Jolt nods toward the ceiling. "We heard a loud noise."

What I've done finally settles over me. They have no idea that their dad is bleeding out in the living room, and I'd like to keep it that way as long as possible. They don't need to see him like that. As I walk down the steps, I tell them the only thing that will make them listen. "Ogier wants you to stay down here to be safe. I'm just here for the girl."

The moment I step off the last stair, I see a child shaking in the old meth tub. The poor thing whimpers beneath her blindfold, shifting uncomfortably in her cord binding.

"What the hell did you little assholes do to her?"

Ignoring me, they're right on my heels, shooting off their questions. "How long?"

"Until we can?"

"Go back upstairs?"

Bolt's fingers clench the edge of the tub, and I think it's the first time I've ever seen his eyes appear so scared. Just looking at him makes me feel like I'm being smashed between two concrete walls. Fuck. Even though shooting Ogier was an accident, I had brought my gun here with that very intention. If Ogier dies, I'll have not only killed someone, I'll have orphaned three children.

"What?"

"Was that?"

"Noise?"

I hold my hand up to stop them. "Just give me a second." Reaching behind the girl's head to untie the rag, I realize her hair is the same bright red shade as Sarah's. She blinks up at me, and when she meets my eyes, my skin goes rigid. That look. It's the same one Sarah gave me the first time I met her. "Are you okay?"

Her face is red and puffy, but otherwise, she seems physically unharmed. She frantically looks between the triplets as I unwrap the cord. "I-I think so."

"We were." Jolt rolls her eyes and crosses her arms.

"Just playing." Bolt grins, giving the girl a wink.

Cask shrugs. "With her."

Kneeling in front of the girl, I ask, "Did Fink bring you here?" Her eyebrows narrow in confusion, so I add, "The man with the cane?" When she nods, she confirms what I knew the moment I saw her eyes. Fink's starting over. That's all Sarah ever really was to him…an experiment. I point a finger to the triplets, "Stay here." As I stand, I place a gentle hand on the girl's back over her dirty nightgown. "Don't be scared, I won't hurt you."

She allows me to guide her upstairs, and I make sure the kitchen is empty before leading her to Ogier's back door. I really hope she can follow directions because the last thing I need is for her to get lost.

"Listen very carefully. I want to help you, but I need you to do exactly as I say, all right?"

Her head nods hard, flopping her matted

red hair around. "All right."

"Go to the street in front of this house and walk left—Wait, you know your left and right… right?"

She frowns at me, deadpanning. "I'm nine and a half."

"Of course. So, you need to walk left until you get to a street called Wingdon. Go right for two streets and you'll reach Nightshade Boulevard. Turn left and my house is the fourth on the right. The gray one with black trim. Go inside and find Sarah. I think you met her earlier." Her eyes widen, and while I suppose I can understand why Sarah's appearance could be discerning for the child, I still have to push back the anger it causes me that this Mundane girl could see her that way. "Don't worry, she's very nice. Wait with her until I get there, okay?"

I gasp, throwing up my hands in shock when she wraps her arms around my thighs. "Thank you," she whispers before spinning around and running outside.

Walking back toward the triplets, I stop before opening the basement door. What the hell am I going to say to them? I can't give them the answers to their questions. They've always looked up to me. After this, they're sure to hate me. I rest my head against the door and slowly turn the lock. I can't do it. Taking a minute to compose myself, I groan at my cowardice then turn back to the mess I've made.

As soon as I cross the threshold into the kitchen, Mayor Greer lunges at me, grabbing my throat to slam me against the wall. "What the fuck, John?!" He has every right to be furious. How the hell am I going to explain my sudden change of heart when not even I understand it? "Do you know the impossible situation you've put me in?!" He's yelling so close to my face his hot breath moistens my cheeks. When I don't respond, he releases me with a growl. I rub the soreness on my neck as he paces the floor. Jabbing a hand to emphasize each word, he orders, "Tell. Me. What. Happened."

"I'm in love with Sarah Stein." The words spew out on their own accord, leaving me gaping at my self-revelation.

His smile is a confused one, clearly unsure if I'm bullshitting him. "But Sarah's…"

"Alive. I know." I shake my head as I walk

over to the kitchen table, falling into the closest chair. "I'm just as surprised as you are." My tense muscles ache as my nerves continue to fray.

He arches a brow, seemingly in an odd limbo over how to feel. "So, what? You find out she's with Ogier, and you decide to storm in here like Rambo, shooting him and beating the piss out of Ingvar? What the hell did you think was going to happen?"

"Shooting Ogier was an accident, and what was I supposed to do? Let Ingvar kick my ass? I didn't come here with a plan, I just had to get her out of here."

He rubs his temples. "Jesus Christ, John. You walked into someone's home uninvited, shot a resident, was violent with another, and according to Fink, you stole from him and Ogier."

"I didn't steal shit. I freed two girls that were here against their will. This town is about giving in to our darkest desires, but that little girl and Sarah were never given a choice. Why are Fink and Ogier's rights more important than theirs?"

His chest rises with his deep inhale.

"Honestly, I have no love lost for Ogier. If I could, I would cover this up and move on, but your dumb ass left a witness, two if Ogier survives. And while I am sympathetic, what you're talking about goes against the way we've been doing things for over a hundred years."

While of course I'd prefer to stop Fink or anyone else from bringing in unwilling Mundaners, I'm also not stupid enough to waste time trying to appeal to Greer's questionable conscience. Instead, I speak in terms he's more likely to understand. "You're right. In fact, it's been exactly one hundred years. There's been a ton of advances in forensic science since Hallows Grove came to be. And I'm sure the Mundaners will use those resources to locate one of their missing children."

He growls as he heads toward the living room. "I could kill you for making me deal with this horse shit."

The paramedics are loading Ogier into the ambulance when we enter. Fink glares at me one last time before following them outside. We don't have a hospital; Fink has the resources to take care of most medical needs in his lab, and there are three or four trained paramedics in town that always help with transportation.

Baron Vendire, the police chief, kneels next to the pool of blood Ogier left behind, using a large turkey baster to suction the crimson liquid from the floor. Once it's almost full, he tilts his head back, squirting a healthy amount into his mouth.

Wiping the red from his lips, he nods to the Mayor. "Fink is taking Ogier back to his lab, says he needs surgery."

Mayor Greer grunts, crossing his arms and looking at me. "Give me some time to talk to Fink and feel out the situation. Where is the Mundane girl?"

I'm nervous to tell him. I'm worried he's going to order that I take her back to Fink, and that sure as hell isn't happening. "She's with Sarah, at my house."

"And what do you suggest we do with her? I do agree with you about her abduction bringing unwanted attention to the town, but it's not as if we can just let her go."

"Why not? I doubt she even knows where she is. Besides, she seems to trust me. I'm confident I can take her home without risking the town any more than Fink already has." I honestly have no idea if I can trust her or not, but I do know she doesn't belong here, and for some reason, it feels like my responsibility to stop the cycle that I allowed Sarah to endure. I can't have the little girl's life on my conscience like Sarah's is.

Mayor Greer growls, balling his hands in to fists. "Goddamn it. Don't do anything until I give you the go ahead." He looks around as if suddenly realizing something. "Where are the Sanity Eaters?"

I gesture my head toward the back of the house. "Still in the basement."

"Get them out of here. The last thing I need is to deal with those little pricks. Take them to their aunts' house, then go home and wait for my call."

Not giving him a chance to change his mind and toss me in the jailhouse, I do as he says. The triplets are huddled together in the tub when I make my way to the bottom of the steps. They all frown at me, falling over each other in their attempts to stand up.

"Tell us."

"What's.

"Happening!"

"Listen…" While I don't know how much information Mayor Greer wants them to have, it's really my own cowardice that keeps me from telling them the truth. "Your dad wants me to take you to your aunts' house. Come on."

Climbing up the stairs, I hear them stomping as they follow. Bolt runs past me, standing on the step above me to block my way. "Where?"

Jolt is right behind him. "Is our?"

Cask tries to stand next to them, but there's not enough room in the stairwell. "Dad?"

An invisible blade turns in my stomach, knowing my actions will soon alter all three of their lives. They may be dick heads, but they're still kids. I push my way through them. "Busy. Now shut up and let's go." Although I feel a bit guilty for talking to them that way after what I've done, if I act any different, they'll know something's up. I don't want them to see the blood stain on the floor in the living room, so I lead them out the back door.

We don't even get to the street before Jolt

starts loading up a slingshot to hit her brothers with. Just getting the few blocks to the sisters' house is a nightmare. Since the boys don't have their own slingshots, they throw rocks at each other, hitting me multiple times in the process.

The Zeldamine Apothecary coming into view makes me sigh in relief. "Oh, thank Christ."

Corralling them all up the steps, I lead them to the apartment and ring the bell. As soon as the door opens, all three of them run past Wanda and Willow to go inside.

I hold my hand out as if it will stop them, even though they're long gone. "God, I'm sorry."

"Is everything all right?" Willow asks, twirling her fingers through her long, gray hair, inspecting my face. Ingvar's fist must've done a number on it from her expression.

Wanda glances over her shoulder at the sound of a *crash*, so I rush out my words before the triplets break more of their stuff.

"Can you watch the Sanity Eaters for a few days? Ogier's... unavailable right now, and I have to deal with some things." They both tilt their heads toward each other. While they appear curious, they also look much more pleased with my request than I'd expected.

"Of course, we love our little devils!" Wanda claps her hands together, the eight rings on her fingers clashing against each other. She's considerably shorter and much stouter than her older sister, though, they both have a very distinct nose, making their resemblance more obvious.

"Thank you. Your next order is on the house."

As soon as I say it, I realize I have no idea if I'm even going to be allowed to live here anymore, but I'll have to cross that bridge when the time comes.

Willow holds up her finger. "Oh, before you go, come with me, dear."

I wave to Wanda in gratitude just as more *bangs* and *crashes* sound from the back of their apartment. Willow leads me downstairs by the hand, telling me to wait outside as she rushes into the store. Seconds later, she returns with a jar and hands it to me.

"For the cuts on your face. We can't have you ruining that pretty thing." Cackling, she winks at me before heading back up the stairs to her apartment.

Her flirting is nothing new, so I chuckle as I read what she gave me. The label says: **Hangman's Salve** *with hemlock and opium*. The products from their apothecary can be pretty hit and miss on whether they actually work or not, but it's worth a shot.

Looking toward the direction of my house, I take a deep breath. I have no idea what's going to happen with the Mundane girl or if Sarah will ever really forgive me. Even with my possible execution or banishment, I can't regret a single decision I made today. While of course, I wish Ogier wouldn't have gotten shot, as long as I can free both girls from more horrors, I'll honestly be at peace with however this turns out.

BATS
Sarah Stein

November 17th ~Midday

STEPPING OUTSIDE WITHOUT HAVING TO SNEAK feels a little strange. It's almost as if the air has been purified. Pushing off my feet, I sprint toward John's house. I'm still reeling from the way he looked at me. It wasn't anything like the last time I saw him. There was no cruelty or self-disgust, just…compassion. He was at Ogier's because of me, that much was clear. Why would he do that if he didn't care about me?

At John's, I'm greeted by an overly excited puppy as soon as I open the door. "Hey, Nothing." My fingers scratch behind his ears when I notice the bags the triplets had earlier.

Fighting my curiosity has never been my strong suit. Nothing sits with his tail wagging as I open the first bag.

A couple of small Styrofoam boxes sit on top of something flat wrapped in brown paper. I pick up the smallest box and take off the lid, immediately almost dropping it with my scream.

Eyeballs. Two bright blue eyeballs stare up at me.

The second I make the connection as to whom these eyes belong to, I gasp so loudly with my sob that I startle Nothing.

Esty. My hands shake so badly, I have to dig my fingers into my palms to keep from dropping the bags. I refuse to let anyone turn her into a prop or a piece of furniture.

Careful to not bump anything, I carry them into John's backyard. Once I find a shovel, I set to digging, only to find the ground is too hard for me to get very deep. Through tear blurred vision, I hide the bags beneath the back-porch steps.

Nothing's collar *jingles* as he follows me back into the house. I sit on the couch in the parlor, tapping my fingers on the armrest. When John gets back, I'll ask him to help me bury Esty. Maybe even in the Hallows Grove Cemetery. I think she'd like it there, it's quiet. I wipe my tears and take a big breath. I wish I could have been friends with her, though, it does ease the sadness knowing that nobody else can hurt her anymore.

My boredom becomes overwhelming, and I eventually give into it when I get up to walk around his house. Curiosity itches my fingertips when I reach for the door that leads downstairs to his workshop. He's shown it to me before, so I doubt he'll mind my exploring.

I pull the string that turns on the light before descending the steps. Snooping around the room, I stop to look at his implements, running my fingers over the cool metal. Nothing curls up in a bed in the corner as I walk around the workshop. Blood stains the concrete, and large waste bins line the walls. I find a pile of clothing and come across a bright red wig. I didn't know he put wigs on his girls, but why would I?

The rest of the room is already well organized, so I set to folding the clothes into a nice stack when I notice a familiar fabric. Lifting it from the pile, I smile in embarrassment even though the only one here is Nothing. My panties. He kept them just like I'd hoped.

Beneath the last few pieces of clothing, loose pieces of paper peek out. I tug them from under the pile when the skin around my eyes stretches wide with my surprise. It's full of sketches. Sketches of...me.

They're drawn like diagrams, pinpointing important pieces, such as my red hair and mouth wound. He's planning to make a body look like me. A smile that is too strong to push away lifts my lips. I don't understand what he's afraid of, but this proves that he does care. He does want me. I hold the papers close to my chest while I continue exploring.

I've seen a few taxidermized animals around his house, so when I enter what looks like a storage area, I'm not shocked to find rows of bats lining the wall. They range in quality of work, the final one appearing so real, I keep expecting it to take flight. I wonder if that's how he taught himself the art of taxidermy? With bats?

THE DIRTY HEROES COLLECTION

Once I've investigated all there is to see, I sit on the floor next to Nothing and stare at the drawings he created with me in mind.

My fingers stroke over Nothing's ghost white hair when I hear a noise. I stand up, listening closely when a voice so small it couldn't be John's says, "Um…Sarah? Are you here?"

Running up the stairs, I pray it's the little girl who was with Fink. Nothing is on my heels, and the moment I reach the top, relief floods through me in a heavy sigh. "Oh, thank goodness."

Her eyes momentarily widen when she sees me, shifting away as if uncomfortable. "Uh, hi. The Skeleton King told me to come here," she mumbles, looking to Nothing who greets her by licking her hand, nearly making her smile.

I kneel in front of her, feeling sick at the fact that she has red hair like I do. I'm careful to speak as softly as I can because she's trembling from what I'm sure is fear. "I know I look like a scary monster, but I promise, I won't hurt you."

Her gaze slowly lifts to meet mine. "What happened to your face?"

Giving her a smile, I say, "I was hurt by a bad man."

"Me too."

I look over her exposed skin, searching for signs of his blade, wanting to cry with relief when I see there are none. Allowing myself to sit on the floor, I sigh, pointing to my cheek. "I know, he's the same man who did this to me."

Her eyebrows scrunch with her skeptical stare. "The man with the cane?" I nod, and she whispers, "Oh."

While she doesn't seem to be physically wounded, she's completely filthy. "What about a warm bath? Would you like that?"

Clasping her hands together, she quickly answers, "Yes, please."

After searching for the bathroom, I find her a towel and set off to look for something clean she can wear. When I come to what I know is John's bedroom, I feel like I'm where I shouldn't be. It's a struggle, but I successfully fight the urge to snoop as I choose a T-shirt from his drawer.

The little girl carries herself in a much more relaxed way once she's clean. We sit in the living room and wait for John while she plays with Nothing on the floor.

"What's your name?" I ask.

"My real name is Sandy Kloss. But I think I'm supposed to be called Sarah now."

Flashes of memories blink in my brain, impossible to grasp. I don't have a single recollection of him telling me Sarah was my new name. Ever since Fink told me about his daughter, I've been so curious to know what my old name was.

"How did you end up with Fink?"

Looking into her lap, she wrings her hands. "When I was walking home from school yesterday, he stopped me and told me that my mom was hurt. He said that she asked him to bring me to the hospital." Her gaze turns glossy and Nothing must sense something because he curls up closer to her. "He knew my name." I wonder if he took me in a similar way? "I also thought I'd seen him before because he looked familiar. So, I got in his car and then he brought me to his house." Red blooms across her cheeks as her voice breaks. "I don't think there was ever anything wrong with my mom."

I don't want her to cry. Changing the subject, I point to Nothing who's licking her hand. "He seems to really like you."

Sniffling, she wipes her arm across her nose. "What's his name?"

I get on the floor, sitting next to her and scratching his side. "Nothing."

She scrunches her nose, clearly not amused by John's choice. "That's not a very good name."

I laugh when the sound of the door opening launches my heart into my throat. "Stay here," I tell her.

While forcing Nothing to remain in her lap, she nods her understanding. The second I step out of the parlor, I meet John's eyes. I don't know how I'll survive more rejection from him, but at the same time, I won't lose the only man I've ever truly cared for because I'm scared of bruising my pride.

"What's happening?"

"A lot. I'm waiting to hear from Mayor Greer." He looks past my shoulder, worry furrowing his brows. "Where's the girl?"

In my excitement over his return, I just now realize that his face is bloody and beaten. "She's playing with Nothing in the parlor. Are you okay?"

He bites his lower lip as his eyes trail up

and down my body. There are so many things hiding behind his eyes when he looks at me. "I'm fine..." Walking closer, he cups my cheek the moment he reaches me. His mouth lifts in a crooked smile, revealing his left dimple. "Do you want to help me piss off Greer?" Playfulness suddenly radiates off of him, and I wish I could just go along with it. In reality, though, I'm still feeling quite melancholy, and insubordination against the Mayor never ends pleasantly. He must sense my hesitation because the smile falls from his face. "I just want to take the little girl back home."

Invisible weights sit on my hands and feet, making me feel heavy. I want to help her, I really do, but I can't help being angry at the unfairness of her getting to return to her family when I never got the chance. "Her name is Sandy. Sandy Kloss."

Sandy's voice interrupts before I get the chance to respond. "Do I get to go home?"

John breaks our connection as his focus lands on her. "Where is that exactly? Do you know your address?"

Holding up a finger, she says, "Yes. I live at

1225 Elfman Lane in Hollyville."

Kneeling in front of her, he takes her hand. She doesn't even flinch. Whatever he did to save her, she apparently trusts him because of it.

"Can you make me a promise?"

She presses her lips together, hesitant about what she's agreeing to. "I-I think so…"

"When we bring you home, will you keep this place a secret? Not everyone here is like Fink, and it could hurt a lot of nice people if you tell anyone you were here."

She shakes her head in confusion. "That's it?"

"That's it. You can tell whoever you want to about what Fink did, just please don't tell them he took you here."

In a sudden movement that startles Nothing, she wraps her arms around John, nearly knocking him over. "I won't tell, I double swear. All I want is to get back to my mom and dad."

He nods at her. "All right then, let's get you out of here."

John takes out a map to search for Hollyville, which ends up being less than an hour from our town. We all follow him to his car where I sit in front and Sandy sits in the back with Nothing.

Once we get out of Hallows Grove without any trouble and onto the main road, he glances in the rearview.

"Do you have any questions before I drop you off?"

She responds so quickly, it's as if she's been waiting for him to ask. "Why is the doggie's name 'Nothing?'" John and I both grin at the obvious disdain in her voice when she asks this.

He lets out a small laugh. "You're right, it's really not that inspired, is it? The day I got him I was scoping out a gr—" he stops himself, adorably stuttering through his next few words. "A possible...er...um, business location," Sandy raises an eyebrow in skepticism, but he continues, "I saw him playing with a bunch of other puppies in a backyard. He ran right up to the fence, and the little guy wouldn't stop barking until I leaned down to pet him." Sandy grins at Nothing, rubbing his back. "A man came out to see if I was interested in keeping one of the dogs. When I asked him how much they were, the man told me, '*I just need 'em off my hands, so...Nothing.'"* John shrugs with a smirk. "And I don't know, I felt like it fit."

Sandy's lips press together as if considering whether that excuses what she obviously feels is an offensive name. "Oh," is her only response. I don't think she's completely convinced.

We're getting closer, and Sandy must know it because she hasn't stopped looking out the window for a few miles. I hate that she had to spend a single moment away from her family because of me. If I hadn't have given Fink a reason to look for a replacement, she wouldn't have been taken.

I wonder if she'll hate me for that someday.

TRIAL

John Skelver

November 17th ~ Evening

I CAN'T BELIEVE MY EYES AS WE DRIVE BENEATH a huge archway, adorned in garland and Christmas lights that sparkle in the setting sun. 'Welcome to Hollyville' is carved out in large script lettering, removing any doubt that we're in the right place. Synthetic snow is sprinkled along the windows, and not a single building is free of colorful lights. A gigantic tree decorated in ornaments of every shape and color, ribbons, and tinsel sits in what appears to be a town square, topped with a bright, glittering star.

Sarah gasps next to me as we pass cardboard cutouts of snowmen and elves. Giant candy canes line all the streets, and oversized presents with billowing bows are scattered at every corner. Christmas isn't really a big deal in Hallows Grove; we definitely don't decorate for it. It's been years since I've seen embellishments anywhere close to these.

The first signs I see are about a food drive. Then there's more for shelter donations and fundraisers. There aren't gates to keep visitors out like in Hallows Grove, and the amount of people that smile in greeting as we drive to her house is staggering. It's impossible to not wonder what life would be like here. How must it feel to be surrounded by joy and kindness instead of death and darkness?

As whimsical as it is, this place isn't who I am or somewhere I could ever belong. I belong in Hallows Grove with Sarah. I truly believe that. I just hope it's still possible.

Sandy tells me to turn on Elfman Lane, and when I stop my car down the street from her house, I turn in my seat to face her. Even though I didn't have a direct hand in her coming to Hallows Grove, my contribution to the way of life there is a large part of why Fink was able to take her. I'm under no delusion that I truly saved this Mundane girl. I wish I had something to give her that could erase every single event of the last couple days, but I don't. Whatever horrors Fink put her through will corrode her mind and soul with age.

"I know what Fink did to you was probably really scary. Try to not let the bad things he did control your decisions in life, okay? Don't give up the choice to be who you want to be. No matter how hard it is."

I'm not sure if she's old enough to really comprehend what I mean, yet from the expression on Sarah's face, she understands completely.

"Uh…okay," Sandy says as she looks out the window toward her house. It's clear how badly she's longing to go inside.

Nodding toward the cute, little, white trimmed house, I smile at her. "Go on, Sandy Kloss. Try to forget us if you can."

She startles me, just as she did the first time when she leans forward, reaching between the seats to wrap her arms around my neck.

"I could never forget you. Thank you,

Skeleton King." Sarah holds her hand up in a wave, her smile making me curious as to why it's so sad. Releasing me from her hold, Sandy grins big enough to show teeth. "Bye, Sarah"

"Bye, Sandy." Sandy swings open the door, sprinting down the street. "Do you think she'll say anything?" Sarah asks as I put the car in drive.

It may be stupid and risky trusting a child with our fate, yet something tells me she'll keep our secret. "I guess we'll see." I want to reach over and hold her hand, but I don't. Even though she doesn't seem as angry anymore, it doesn't mean she's forgiven me.

"Are you okay?"

A slow breath slithers from her lips, and she's quiet for so long, I assume she's choosing to ignore me. Maybe she's still pissed.

"I'm…" She exhales a deep breath. "I wonder if I came from somewhere like Hollyville. Maybe I had parents that were sad when Fink took me away." Lacing her fingers, she looks over to me. "I wish I could remember what my real name was."

To a degree, I understand why she wants to

know her origins, I just can't relate. I've spent my entire life trying to forget mine. Just thinking about not wanting to remember forces me to.

The twelve minutes must have passed by now. My entire body feels weak and numb. Just as I'm about to give up and fall to the ground, Mom opens the back door.

"Get inside and stand in the kitchen."

Her disgusted expression has only worsened during our time apart. Not giving her a chance to take back her offer, I shuffle inside as quickly as I can without being able to feel my feet. The heated house is almost too much with the extreme change my skin is experiencing. I've been standing in the kitchen for only a few seconds when she comes in after me. I wish she would let me get dressed. It's mortifying to be naked beneath her gaze.

She stands in front of me with her hands behind her back. My entire body is shaking uncontrollably, my teeth chattering loud in my ears.

"Clasp your hands at the small of your back, and keep them there." Her voice is so harsh, void of any comfort, making me wonder if she's always despised me. Has her hate been growing over the years?

My palms sweat and my cheeks burn as I hold my hands behind my back, revealing my genitals. "Self-pollution is one of the lowest forms of perversion. You spoil your mind and soul every time you lust after yourself, and I refuse to allow such disgusting behavior in my home. You will not be a man like your father." I flinch like I do every time she compares us. "Close your eyes, or don't, but the second you move your hands, I start over."

She reveals the stick she's been hiding behind her back, making it hard to catch my breath with the short and rapid tempo my lungs are expanding at. My throat goes dry as my frosty skin beads with sweat. When she brings her arm back, I tense, squeezing my eyes shut.

"AAHHHH!" The scream rips from my throat. I never could have imagined this would be so excruciating.

"One!" my mother barks.

Fuck, fuck, fuck. eleven more to go. For as long as I can remember, whatever my punishment has been, it's always coincided with my age. I don't know if I can survive one more let alone eleven.

I can't pry my eyes open or stop screaming after she switches my flaccid penis. It's surely cut and bloody; it feels like she's hacking it off.

It's impossible to lose track of how many strikes I've had with her counting them out loud, and after the seventh one, I can't physically stand up anymore. Falling to my knees, I sob as snot runs from my nose, dripping to the floor.

"Get up." There isn't even a hint of remorse or compassion in her voice over the torture she's putting me through. No indication that she cares at all.

"Mom," I gasp through my tears, "Please, I won't ever do it again, just please stop."

"GET UP, NOW!" Her fingers fist a chunk of my hair to pull me to my feet. "You made the conscious decision to sully yourself in this house knowing full well how nauseatingly sinful it is. Now, stand up straight, and pay your penance."

Bleeding scratches are scattered along my burning shaft, and I close my eyes again. If I get through this, I swear, I will never touch myself again.

The next several seconds are agonizing. Each hit only further magnifying the pain. Cries of torment continuously pour from my lips until she finally announces, "Twelve!"

Relief and overwhelming agony swirl around each other, bringing me to my knees. Leaving me to *cry in a fetal position on the kitchen floor, she walks away, her shoes* clacking *against the linoleum.*

I'm so lost in the burning between my legs that I barely notice when she returns. "If I ever catch you fondling yourself again, I will take even harsher measures that will have you begging for the switch."

I look up to see her light a match, bringing it to the magazine and setting it aflame. She watches it burn before dropping it into the sink and turning on the faucet.

After she washes and dries her hands, she snaps her fingers toward my room. "Get dressed, and get in bed."

Even walking is excruciating. I want so badly to cup my injured genitalia, but there's no way I'd let her see my hands anywhere near there. With gentle caution, I obey what she says, crawling in between the bed sheets once my pajama pants are on.

Right when I think this horrible night is finally over, my door opens, and she walks in with a long, flat board and some rope from the garage. "Sit up," she orders. The second I sit upright, she lays the board flat on the bed. "Lie back down." I'm completely confused about what she's doing until she ties my arms to the board like I'm on a cross. "Twelve nights.

After that, you will have to prove to me that I can trust you." Once my arms are no longer of use, she binds my feet with the remaining rope.

Walking to my light to turn it off, she looks over her shoulder. "I'm not the only one you're a disappointment to. You need to pray for Jesus to help you with these urges, and that He will cleanse your filthy mind."

Slamming the door, she leaves me in the dark.

Not really knowing the best way to respond, I lamely say, "I'm sorry."

Her eyebrow raises as she turns her body to face me. "For what, exactly? What Fink took from me, or what *you* did?" she snaps.

My mouth falls open as she clears her throat and settles back into her seat. "I…" I grip the wheel, growling in frustration under my breath. I don't know how to do this, what to say. "I never wanted to hurt you, Sarah. That night was a lot for me, and I went into self-preservation mode."

"What are you protecting yourself from?" she asks, turning her head to the side.

After everything, at the very least, I owe her honesty. "My life before Hallows Grove wasn't a glamorous one. I was so different from everyone else where I lived. They all despised me—even my own parents. I think I'm ultimately terrified of being unwanted. I swear to you, our night together was easily the best one of my entire life, but fearing the day when you really see who I am was too much. Letting you go felt easier than being hurt."

Contradictory tears fill her eyes despite the sweet smile on her face. "Will you pull over?"

As soon as I put the car in park, her lips are on mine. Regardless of her kiss catching me off guard, I melt into it. Touching her skin again sends bolts of energy through my every nerve ending.

She tells Nothing to get in the back seat as her fingers tug at my jeans, undoing the button. Her kisses move down my neck while her hot hand slips into my underwear to grasp my extremely solid erection, setting my flesh on fire. "I won't ever turn you away, and I won't ever leave," I groan at the increasing movement of her palm, "because I do see who you truly are, John. It's you that can't."

Nobody has ever spoken to me this way,

and it's a little overwhelming. Grabbing her face, I kiss her hard. I can't believe this is happening again. Of course I'm still hesitant and terrified, though, for the first time, the hope that her words are true overpowers my fear. She straddles me, her fingers wrapping around the hem of her dress to reveal that she isn't wearing panties.

"I want to feel you again, and I don't want to wait to get back to Hallows Grove." Fuck. She really does hold the power to obliterate me. "I won't ever change my mind about you. I promise."

I'm too weak to ever be able to turn her away again, no matter how scared I am. Taking my hand, she wraps it around my cock, as if wanting me to guide myself.

The moment my sensitive tip meets her entrance, I push as hard as I can, her gasping at the intrusion somehow makes me even harder. This ecstasy is something that doesn't exist aside from Sarah. Every thrust gets me deeper and makes her hold me closer. She grasps my shoulders while she rotates her hips in a way that has me digging my fingernails into her supple flesh.

Without shame or regret, we use each other's bodi es to drown in euphoria. I want so badly to tell her I love her, but I can't make the words separate from my tongue.

When she comes, fluid expels from her body in spurts, soaking me and my seat in the process. She gets shy and embarrassed about her orgasms, but I don't know why. Clearly, she doesn't know how fucking sexy she looks when she's overcome by pleasure.

She comes down off the high of her orgasm, looking down at her mess in mortification. I grab her face, attempting to kiss away her insecurity. My own body tenses with building pressure, washing over me with tingling currents. "God, you feel so fucking amazing." I moan, releasing inside of her hot body.

We stare at each other, panting. Her cheeks are pink as she smiles at me, and I'm not sure what I'm supposed to say. 'Thank you' doesn't feel right.

Her hands softly touch my cheeks. "Do you believe me now? I don't want you to be scared anymore."

I nod because I do. At least, I want to. It's not fair to not trust her when she's done nothing other than try to prove her devotion. The truth is that the problem lies within me and has for most of my life.

She climbs off of me to buckle her seatbelt which Nothing takes as an invitation to jump into her lap, his tail *thumping* against the dashboard in excitement.

Putting the car in drive, I check to make sure the road is clear of traffic before pulling off the shoulder. "Mayor Greer will be even more pissed if he finds out I left, so we should get back home."

When I released her from Ogier, the thought of her staying with me hadn't even crossed my mind. All I knew was that I needed her away from there. Now, though, I can't think of anywhere else she'd stay, and imagining her warmth lying next to me every single night excites me in an unfamiliar way.

"What's happening?"

Her question rips me from my fantasies. "What?"

Looking through my cassette tapes, she

picks Pearl Jam's *Ten* and opens it up to read the insert. "At your house, you said that you were waiting on Mayor Greer. Waiting on him for what?"

Her hand feels so perfect inside my own when I take it, squeezing it to remind myself this is really happening, she's really here. "I broke a lot of the laws that Hallows Grove was founded on. I have no idea what he'll decide to do to me. Not to mention, taking Sandy back before his go ahead went directly against his orders."

She glances out the window, silent a few moments before asking, "If they send you away…can I come with you?"

The grin pulling at my cheeks is impossible to wipe from my face. Life outside of Hallows Grove might not be so scary if she were with me. "You would do that?"

She giggles softly as her cheeks turn rosy. "That's what I've been trying to tell you. I just want to be wherever you are."

Rubbing the back of my neck, I release my own bashful chuckle. "I want to be wherever you are too. I just hope my contribution to Hallows Grove is seen as an important enough resource that I'll be allowed to stay."

I pull up to the south gates and enter my passcode as her body stiffens, still as stone. My stomach flops around in my gut when she pulls her hand away to cross her arms. It's natural to think she realized something about me that she's disgusted by, but if I'm trying to learn how to be with her, I have to ask. "What's wrong?"

She doesn't move for some time, her mouth pressed in a hard line. It isn't until we're in my driveway that she finally answers. "I just told you I wanted to be with you, that I'll never leave no matter what, yet you still plan on being with them, don't you? The dead girls."

It's obvious that she's really upset, so I feel guilty when I can't control my smile. She's jealous. Not only does she want me, she wants me all to herself. I hold back my laugh. Now that I've had her, the real her, I doubt a corpse would do anything for me.

I grasp the back of her neck to make her look at me. "You've ruined the dead for me, Sarah. I'll never desire them as long as you're in my bed. However, for now anyway, I still run a business that requires cadavers. I'm still

Skeleton King." The softening of her features initiates the hardening of my cock. I nod toward the house. "Come on. Let's go inside."

Her voice sounds exasperated when she says, "Wait." When I look at her, she nods toward the backyard. "I need your help with something."

She takes my hand, Nothing following us as she leads me to the back porch. Kneeling down, she points. "The girl in these bags was my…" her eyes shift up for a moment before finishing, "she was my friend. I don't want you to sell her pieces off. I want to bury her. She deserves more than becoming someone's nightstand."

My eyes travel beneath the steps to see the bags the Sanity Eaters brought me. I have questions, that much is for sure, but the look in her eyes tells me I'll need to ask them at a later date. Her friend will never know about any of this, so I don't personally understand why this means so much to Sarah, but I don't need to comprehend it. All that matters is that it's important to her.

"Of course. Do you know where? You want to bury her, I mean?"

She softly takes in a breath. "Could we do it in town? At the cemetery?"

There are still a few plots left since almost everyone in town who has died in the last thirty years has been cremated. "Let me talk to Mayor Greer. I'm sure he'll be fine with it. Until then, it's cold enough out here that she'll be fine for a few days."

Once again, she gives me one of her heartbroken smiles. "Thank you. I think she would've liked that."

Sarah and Nothing follow me inside, and as soon as we reach the parlor, his ears perk up right before my doorbell rings. Sarah freezes, instinctively reaching for Nothing.

"Stay here, and be quiet," I whisper, holding a finger to my lips.

There are only a few people this could be, and I pray it's not the Vendire brothers coming to lock me up. Opening the door allows me a small amount of relief, though, for how long remains to be seen. Mayor Greer stands on my doorstep, looking a little worse for wear.

He barely lets me verbalize my greeting before his words flood out of him. "Fink's been able to stabilize Ogier, but he's still in a coma," he takes a deep breath before snapping, "and since he has a fucking gunshot wound, taking him to a hospital is out of the question."

I feel like I'm always either being praised or chastised by Mayor Greer and there's never an in between. "Would you like to come in?"

He shuffles inside while I close the door. When I turn back to him, I see Sarah's head peeking around the corner. So much for staying put. He barely skips a beat. "I think I have Fink calmed down for the time being, but he's more pissed at you than I am." Glancing to Sarah, he nods to her. "Hello there, sweetheart."

With her cover blown, she shows herself, meeting us in the entryway. "Hello, Mayor."

He turns back to me, pushing his disheveled hair from his face. "Where's the Mundane girl?" Sarah and I glance at each other as an awkward laugh tumbles from my mouth. His lips press together as his bushy brows push toward his nose. "What?"

My cheeks puff with me holding my breath before I blow the air out and rip off the Band-Aid. "I took her back...to her family."

Blinking a few times, he balls up his fists, his body visibly tensing as his face takes on a bright shade of red seconds before erupting. "YOU FUCKING WHAT?!" He's trembling in fury, and I don't know if speaking would help or hurt my cause at this point. "She was the only thing that was going to keep Fink's mouth shut! And what happens when she leads the Mundane police right to us?! I have no power to stop them if they have a warrant, you fool!"

"She promised me she wouldn't." It sounds like a pretty flimsy safety net now that I'm saying it out loud.

He scoffs, growling as he paces the floor. "You better be right because if she does end up running her mouth, we're all completely fucked. Fink wants a trial, and honestly, John, he has every right to one." Shaking his head, he throws his hands up in exasperation. "Without the child, he won't budge. You've brought this on yourself." He turns to leave before adding over his shoulder. "You're on house arrest until further notice. I'll be in touch."

I exhale a large breath, falling back to lean against the wall as he slams the door behind him. Sarah steps in front of me. "What happens at a trial?"

They are rare. I've only ever seen a few, and they never ended well for the accused. "I'll present my case to the town, and Fink will explain his side. Then the town votes."

She worries her lip while resting her warm hands against my chest. "Votes on what?"

Fear settles over me as I realize being exiled is now the least of my worries. "If I'm guilty or not."

With wide eyes, she speaks in a cracked voice. "What if they vote that you're guilty?"

Holding my hand against the back of her head, I hug her against me. "Then they decide whether to take my residency, my freedom, or…" I shrug to lighten the blow, "my life."

November 18th ~ Morning

BEFORE I OPEN MY EYES, I SAVOR THE FEEL OF Sarah's heated body wrapped around me. She's barely taken her hands off me since learning about the trial. My cock hardens beneath the sheets, and I wonder if she'll ever stop having this insatiable effect on me.

Slowly lifting her arm from my chest, I carefully slip from the bed so I don't wake her. Nothing's nails *tap* on the floor as he follows me to the kitchen. I put the coffee on before getting the eggs boiling in a pot.

Sarah walks in just as the bagels pop out of the toaster, wearing my button-down shirt and rubbing her sleepy eyes. The sunlight shines through her red hair, creating a halo effect. I still can't believe she's really here.

While feeling her lifeforce is intense and jarring, I'm becoming more accustomed to it. The moment she walks around the counter, I grab her waist, pulling her in for a kiss. "Good morning."

Her lips quirk as her cheeks turn crimson. "Good morning." Taking one hand from her waist, I reach over to turn off the stove and remove the eggs.

"Do you like coffee?"

She glances at the coffee pot with a shake of her head. "I'm not allowed to have caffeine."

Something clicks in her mind making a grin take over her face. "Well, I wasn't, but now I guess I can have anything I want! So, sure, I'll try it."

Fink has controlled every aspect of her existence for more than half her life. Seeing the excitement on her face because she's free from that, makes my chest feel strained, as if my heart is actually growing larger.

She's not the only one experiencing new things for the first time.

Lifting her up on the edge of the counter, I stand between her open legs to gently touch our mouths together. As much as I want to trust everything that she's told me, old habits die hard. Every kiss is terrifying when I think about the possibility of it being the last.

"I've been curious about something." Slowly pushing my T-shirt up her thighs, I allow my lips to travel down her neck.

"What?" she whispers, her hot breath releasing in puffs against my cheek.

She makes me brave, and I'm elated by that power when my fingers slide inside of her hot entrance. "What you taste like."

I've eaten dead pussy once or twice, but it

was disgusting and did nothing for me. This is different. I want to taste the juices that come out of her when she comes.

Dead girls never come.

Lowering to my knees, I'm face to face with her already wet cunt. I continue to pump my finger, and when I add a second one, she grabs her knees to open herself up to me. Whenever she shows me what she likes, she focuses my touch on her clit, so it would make sense that the same will apply to my tongue. I lick at the little bump, not sure how much pressure or how fast I should go. It doesn't take long before her hands are tugging on my hair, shocking me at how hard that makes my dick twitch.

"Right there, John. Keep doing what you're doing—Oh, God." She writhes against my face, softly moaning her arousal. I can't believe how insane this is. I never would have guessed giving pleasure was just as much fun as receiving it... if not more. The faster her hips thrust, the more aggressive I get with my fingers and tongue.

As she cries out, her fluid expels down my face and neck. Even though it makes it difficult to breathe, I don't stop until I'm drenched and she's pushing my head away. A grin raises her lips as she heaves, watching me stand.

"You're really good at that."

She's so fucking beautiful. My palms force down my sweats as fast as they can. Her fist wraps around my shaft the very moment it's free, making my heart pound. Guiding me inside her, she whimpers against my neck as I stretch her body. I squeeze her ass, pushing myself deeper.

I don't know if I'll ever stop being scared that she'll change her mind about me someday, but in these moments with her, I'm convinced they're worth the fear.

November 18th ~ Afternoon

I THINK TODAY HAS BEEN THE MOST PEACEFUL DAY I've ever had. No corpses, no graveyards, just playing Operation and drinking coffee with Sarah. Coffee that requires four scoops of sugar and a ton of milk for her to drink, apparently. Her laugh is a sound I've heard so many times today. I swear it's made the room visibly brighter. Things between us seem so easy, so natural that I'm almost superstitious enough to believe that maybe we were supposed to be together all along.

Her tweezers touch the edge again, making the buzzer go off and the nose light up. "Darn it!" She clenches her fists in frustration. "That stupid piece of bread is impossible!"

Sincerely laughing gives me a floating feeling that I've felt so rarely in my life. As I take the tweezers from her, the sound of my phone ringing drifts through the house. "Hold on."

In the kitchen, I take the phone off the receiver. "Hello?"

"Tonight's the night," Mayor Greer's gruff voice announces without so much as a greeting. "Soon, I'll alert the town of the meeting. We won't inform them of the trial until everyone has arrived." He sighs in my ear. "You should know, I have your back, son. My testimony will be on your behalf."

Air rushes out of my lungs at his comment. The Mayor's testimony can have a profound impact on the town's final decision. "Thank you, Mayor Greer." Sarah walks into the kitchen with Nothing and leans against the doorframe with curiosity distorting her features.

"Be at the Old Town Hall at seven. The trial will start at seven-thirty. And it might be a good idea to wear the paint. Remind them who you are and why they need you."

I nod, even though he can't see me. "I will."

"All right then. We'll talk tonight."

Sarah's arms wrap around my waist as I hang up the phone. "Is everything okay?"

Kissing her head, I hold her closer. "It's happening. The trial."

She looks up at me with that scared and sad expression she gives me every time the trial is mentioned. "Tonight?"

Nodding toward the parlor, I attempt to change the subject. "Come on, I have a game to beat you at."

Her hair flops around as she shakes her head. "I don't want to play anymore." She takes my hand, and I allow her to lead me up the spiral staircase.

Every kiss, every touch is soaked in desperation. She falls to her knees, frantically

THE DIRTY HEROES COLLECTION

undoing my pants to take me into her hot mouth. I wrap my hands in her hair and close my eyes while memorizing every impeccable sensation. I've been so scared that she would one day, despise me and walk away, when in reality, it might be me who has to leave.

Taking her arm, I lift her to her feet, kissing her as I back us toward the bed. I undress her slowly, reveling in every detail. Scars are scattered across her pale skin, her rosebud nipples rising with each intake of oxygen. The beauty of watching her breathe is so erotic to me.

I lay her on the bed, refusing to take my lips off her skin. She claws at my back the moment I slide inside of her. She's so wet, her body consuming mine in earnest. Her quiet gasps fill my ear, and I can't believe this could be it. The last time I ever hear her breathing, feel her warmth encasing me. It's an intense feeling to be fully accepted and loved for exactly who I am. She chose me, and I don't know how to ever repay her for that. Or if I'll even have the chance to.

It's odd that I'm less scared about being

hanged than I am about losing her. At least if I'm dead, I won't know what I'm missing. She would, though, and while I can't stand the thought of hurting her more, knowing that she would mourn me has my hips thrusting harder, driving me deeper.

I force myself to slow down because I need this to last as long as possible. Pulling out of her, I kiss down her chest and stomach before settling between her legs. I'm slow and soft with my tongue, taking my time, indulging in her taste.

Though I know it was my choices that brought us here, it's still so unfair that I could lose her when it feels like I just found her.

Her fingers are soft as they trail down my arm, her head resting on my chest. "Are you scared?" she whispers. "About tonight?"

I move the hair covering her eye, reminding myself that I can be honest with her. Sighing, I lift her chin. "The only thing I'm scared of is losing you." Her eyebrows crease when she pushes up on her arms to kiss me. When she pulls away, the words lurch from my throat in a frantic whisper. "I love you."

Her eyes widen before her lips lift into a grin. My chest instantly throbs in pain. It literally feels like my heart is ripping down the middle. She giggles, and the rage burns in my gut, waiting to bubble up to the surface. She's mocking me. I don't understand…after everything, why would she—

Cutting off my thoughts, her mouth crashes to mine as she hugs her arms around my neck. "I've loved you since I was nine years old. All I've ever wanted was to hear you say that."

Every dark and damaging thought festering in my mind evaporates the moment I process her words. Expelling a relieved breath loosens my every muscle, and my own grin raises my cheeks. I hold her hand, kissing every scar on every finger as I tell myself once again that she's trustworthy. So many years were spent overlooking her. I can't believe I allowed her abuse every single day, knowing it was happening just down the street.

"I need you to know, I will always regret not

stopping Fink the very first day I met you."

"John, there's nothing you could have—"

"Yes, there was. I could have stood up to him. I could have talked to Mayor Greer about kidnapping kids being a step too far. There is a lot I could have done, and the truth is, there's no excuse. I hid behind fear and my own best interests while telling myself it wasn't my place. I am so, so sorry for that."

She sits up with a smile. "I never thought that was your responsibility, John. Besides, if you had, we wouldn't be here, together."

"Which is more than I deserve." Shifting to throw my legs over the edge of the bed, I feel her hand wrap around my arm.

When I look at her, she cups my face and whispers, "You deserve everything you've ever wanted."

She's so...intense. There's never been anyone in my life to affect me on every level—emotionally, mentally, physically—like she does.

I kiss her forehead before reaching down for her dress. Sometimes she strikes me dumb with her kindness, her...love. I can't think of anything profound to say. "Come on. We should probably eat something before I need to start getting ready."

We go downstairs, and I leave her in the parlor with Nothing to make dinner. When I return with chicken and rice, I find her staring at the television wearing a frown. "Was this you?"

Handing her the plate, I turn toward the TV to see the news playing, immediately recognizing they're filming at the graveyard where I took Wendy. A blonde, middle-aged woman cries into the camera, saying she's her mother.

Please, the woman begs. *Please return her body. Whoever you are, whatever your reasons... We won't look for you or press charges, just please bring us back our baby, and let her rest peacefully.*

My lungs deflate, refusing to circulate oxygen as my mouth drops open, and I slowly sit next to Sarah. The woman looks so...defeated.

She asks me again, "John? Was this one of your girls?"

I nod, trying to swallow as I remember dumping Wendy on my back porch as if she were nothing more than spoiled food.

"Wendy."

"She looks so sad." Sarah's voice is filled with sorrow, and I can't understand how she so easily feels for someone she's never met. I honestly hadn't thought that what I did had any effect on the living.

When my mother died, I didn't see her body as her anymore. The person she was had disappeared, her skin just a vessel that served as a mode of transportation for her essence while she was alive. Our essence is what makes us who we are, what matters most. I've never considered the fact that not everyone feels that way.

"I...I didn't think I was hurting anyone." My appetite has suddenly vanished, so I set my plate on the coffee table.

Sarah leans back against the couch, swallowing a bite of rice. "Maybe you could apologize?"

Crossing my arms, I tilt my head, genuinely curious about her suggestion. "And how the hell would I do that?"

"Do you remember all the girls you've had? Where their graves are?"

There's no way I could ever remember all the bodies I've acquired for pay, yet those I spent intimate time with have burned their way into my brain. "Yes. All of them."

"What if you wrote apology letters to all their families and left them at the empty graves? Tell them you're sorry and that their loved ones are at peace."

"Are they, though?"

She shrugs. "I don't know, but I don't think that's what matters. As long as it makes them feel better."

I don't know how my heart will ever survive her as it swells in my chest. "You're really smart, you know that?"

With her scarred cheeks blushing, she turns her head and smirks. "Well, you're the first to say it."

She doesn't eat much of her food, however, I have no idea how much Fink used to allow her to consume on a daily basis.

Reeeee er reeee. Reeeee er reeee.

The town siren wails ominously around us. *"Town meeting! Town meeting in one hour at the Old Town Hall. Town meeting!"* Mayor Greer's voice floats in through the windows as Nothing tucks his head between his legs and hides under the couch. He's always hated that fucking siren.

The Mayor's voice magnifies through his megaphone as I pick up our plates and stand to my feet. "I need to shower and try to figure out what the hell I'm going to say. You can watch TV or read a book, whatever you'd like." She nods, reaching under the couch to comfort Nothing.

After I shower, I put on my skull face. And while it stings like a bitch around my cuts and bruises from my fight with Ingvar, I'm glad Mayor Greer made the suggestion. I'm always more confident with it on. It takes forever to apply the greasepaint, so when I finally finish, it's nearly time to leave.

Sarah's on the floor in the parlor playing tug-o-war with Nothing and his rope. I scratch his ear before taking her hand to pull her to her feet. "I'm going to get going. I'll see you there, okay?" She smiles, staring at my lips. Leaning down, I kiss her, still stunned that I'm able to do so with a willing, living girl. And not just any girl...with Sarah Stein. Slowly separating our hands, I walk to the door before adding, "Be sure to stay away from Fink."

Tilting her head with an unamused expression, she deadpans, "Obviously."

Grinning, I walk outside, wondering how she survived him all these years with her snark.

The closer I get to Old Town Hall, the more I feel like I'm about to have a panic attack. My heartbeat sounds like a drumline, my guts are tied up in a slipknot, and I'm sweating my ass off. This night could end with a noose around my neck or worse. There have been times when the winner was given the opportunity to choose the loser's fate. I've seen a woman buried alive and a man flayed to death. I left that part out while telling Sarah about trials because I didn't want to make her more upset than she already was.

Mayor Greer is getting out of his gray, vintage pick-up truck as I'm walking up the steps. "Are you ready?"

"As ready as I'll ever be, I suppose."

He grunts, pulling open the Town Hall doors for us. "I want to keep you separated from Fink until the trial begins." He leads me to a conference room and gestures to a seat. "I suggest using this time to think about the points you want to make if you haven't already. I'll be back in a few minutes."

The door slams behind him, the quietness of the room allowing me to hear the pronounced *click* of the lock being put into place. I stare at the clock on the wall, watching the second hand ticking closer and closer to my possible demise. I'd love to be confident that the people in this town are my friends and would never sentence me to death for saving the girl that I love. That's my main defense; I did everything because I love Sarah. And there's no doubt in my mind I'd do it again. Today was easily the best day of my life, and it never would have happened without the choices I made.

If things don't go in my favor tonight, I don't know if I'll be allowed to talk to Sarah one last time. I regret not thanking her for everything she's given me and wish I'd told her that I've never loved anyone the way I love her. I would also ask her to take care of Nothing and make sure he doesn't just eat treats.

Before I know it, Mayor Greer is unlocking the door. "Okay, John, it's time." Straightening my jacket, I follow him into the main auditorium. "Fink will give his testimony first, then you'll speak. Sarah will be next, then I will give my assessment of the situation."

What?! My head jerks in his direction as I ask a little louder than intended, "Sarah is testifying?"

His eyes narrow, reminding me to compose myself before I piss off the man trying to help me. "This is a good thing. She'll help your case."

Maybe. Or this could go south and she'll be branded a traitor.

Word must have gotten out about what this meeting is about because the rows are fuller than I've ever seen them. Murmurs dance across the crowd as I take my seat behind the pulpit on the opposite side of Fink. I spot Sarah in the front row with Nothing, giving me a sweet smile. I shake my head, in a pathetic attempt to dissuade her from speaking. She clearly understands my meaning when she defiantly nods her head yes.

Her stubbornness frustrates the fuck out of me, yet at the same time I can't help but be proud of her for her bravery. I'm learning that being in a relationship with someone that can speak and feel is extremely complicated. I've also learned how important trusting her is for my sanity. I have to believe she knows what she's doing.

Mayor Greer takes his place behind the pulpit as the room falls silent. "As I'm sure many of you have heard, this meeting has been called to serve as the trial for Johnathan 'Skeleton King' Tarik Skelver. I request that you stay silent until all testimonies have been heard. Once all parties have spoken, you will be given the opportunity to ask any questions you may have. You will then be allotted the time to fill out the ballots you received when you arrived. Officers Baron and Lestar Vendire will take them from you when you leave." Gesturing to Fink, he says, "First we'll hear from Franklin 'Fink' Reginald Stein who feels he was wronged by the accused."

Mayor Greer steps away from the pulpit to allow Fink to address the town. Resting his cane against the podium, he uses it for support.

"Good evening. Most of you have known me and my family for many years. My father, grandfather, and great-grandfather were all scientists with unconventional methods, and I am no different." His fingers squeeze the edge of the podium. "As I'm sure you've heard at one point or another, I attempted life in the Mundane World after I fell in love and started a family. Unfortunately, that all came to a horrific end, and I truly hope none of you will ever know the pain of losing a child like I did. When I found Sarah and brought her here to Hallows Grove, it was the first time I felt that I could really heal from my loss."

I bite my lip because this isn't supposed to be a debate. I'll get my chance to speak, but what about Sarah? Yes, he felt he was able to heal, but he did so by pushing his pain on to someone else, giving her no choice in the matter. She was completely innocent.

"John is here because of me. I brought him into the folds of our utopia, so maybe some of the fault is on me for thinking he was trustworthy. He has known everything about me and Sarah since I brought her here and has never once stated an opinion on the matter. If you know Sarah, you know she can be stubborn and insubordinate."

I glance at Sarah whose face is twisted into

fury. She has earned every ounce of her rage, and I'm suddenly glad she's going to speak. If anyone has a right to share their side, it's her.

"I tried. For the past decade I did everything in my power to show Sarah that I loved her. But in the end, I wasn't enough." He has the audacity to look like she hurt him, as if he's the victim in this macabre tale. "It hurt me greatly to make the choice to move on from her, but I needed someone that loved me as much as I did them. Sarah was clearly unhappy, and Ogier had the desire to take care of her. Because I still love her, I let her go, deciding to start over in my search for someone who could replace the daughter I lost. And I found someone, a beautiful girl that could give me what Sarah wouldn't."

While I can't tell how the residents are reacting to his confession, I do know they have history with his bloodline. I, unfortunately, have no such connection.

"Ogier Oliviar Bognar and I made a fair and just arrangement when it came to Sarah, however, John Skelver interjected himself in our business deal. A deal he was in no way a part of. I was an invited guest in Ogier's home yesterday when John barged in without permission, threatening us both at gunpoint. This from a man I'd thought was my friend. If we can't be safe and secure here, in Hallows Grove, then where is the sanctuary where we can?" Whispers and murmurs are exchanged between residents as he continues, "When we would not fold to his outlandish demands, John shot Ogier and beat Ingvar so badly he's still in extensive pain. Yet that wasn't enough for him, apparently. He then proceeded to take not only Sarah from Ogier but my new daughter and my only chance at sanity from me. Besides being a traitor and possibly a murderer, John Skelver also broke one of our most sacred rules. He treated me as if I were a degenerate, shaming me for my lifestyle. Here. The one place where we should all be accepted for who we are. My suggestion is death by dismemberment." Sarah jumps from her seat, opening her mouth as if to say something when she must recall Mayor Greer's instructions about staying silent, abruptly sitting back down. "I believe he should be physically torn apart since he has emotionally done the same to me. Ogier is still fighting for his life and is currently in a coma. If he dies, John will have killed a respected member of this community while simultaneously orphaning three children." Clasping his hands together, he nods to the crowd. "Thank you for your time. I'm confident that all of you will make the right choice." He picks up his cane, glaring at me as he hobbles back to his seat.

Mayor Greer returns to the podium. "Thank you, Franklin. Now it's time we hear from the accused." He turns to me, gesturing to the pulpit. "John, you may now explain your version of these events."

I stand on rubber legs, presenting myself to the entire town. "Hello everyone, thank you for being here."

Looking down at Sarah, I'm reminded of what I have to lose. If I'm voted guilty, regardless of the punishment, what will happen to her? Will they make her go back to Fink? She nods to me, and I swallow.

"Franklin is right. I haven't been a member of Hallows Grove for very long in comparison to most of you. My family has no ties to this place. I'm here because of him, and I'll always be grateful for that. And yes, I did stand by for years knowing what he did to Sarah. I told myself that I had no room to intervene, and truthfully, I just tried to ignore it. Let's be honest, though, we all know what his 'love' consisted of. You can see her scars, and there are many more you can't see."

It's hard to get a read on what the spectators are thinking. Some appear angry while others don't show any sign of emotion. "I believe in this town and what it stands for. This is my home. We all should have a place where we can be free and safe, but what about Sarah? She was never given a choice. He took her from her family and brought her here to experiment on. Of course she was unhappy. While I empathize with his pain, the way he's gone about fixing it is…" I shift on my feet, gripping tight to the podium. "Wrong." That gets a reaction, their murmurs rising a few octaves. I can't make out what they're saying, but I don't think it's good. If there's anything that's a sin here it's moral judgement. "I'm not saying I'm blameless, but Sarah is. It took me falling in love with her to truly open my eyes. He's kept her locked away from all of us, and I believe it was to prevent us from seeing her as a person. I don't doubt he has some love for her, it's impossible not to love a person like Sarah, but she deserves the same rights as all of us."

Standing up straight, I give them my confession. "So, yes, when I learned that Fink, Franklin, had given Sarah to Ogier, I felt compelled to save her. You all know what Ogier does to his whores. I went to his house with a gun and the intention to threaten him with it if I had to. What I didn't expect was for Fink to be there. During our confrontation, he ordered Ingvar to attack me, and when he did, the gun went off in my hand. Shooting Ogier was an accident, and I only beat up Ingvar to protect myself. When I found the little Mundane girl Franklin stole to replace Sarah, another child taken from their family, I took the girl home where she belongs."

Sarah holds Nothing back as he keeps trying to come to me onstage. "I may not be a Hallows Grove native, but you all know me. I would never do anything to hurt any of you. Of course I want to stay, to continue being your

Skeleton King, but what I really want to ask of you is to give Sarah her freedom regardless of the outcome of this trial," I plead with them, still having no better idea of how they're feeling. "Thank you for listening, and no matter what happens, I will always be grateful to every single one of you for making this place a home for me the last twelve years."

Returning to my seat, I pass Mayor Greer who gives me a subtle nod, seemingly approving of my statement. "Thank you, John. Next we'll listen to the testimony of Sarah Elizabeth Stein who has requested to speak on John's behalf." He waves her on. "Come on up, sweetheart."

As soon as she stands, Nothing sprints onto the stage to sit next to me. I'm grateful for it because this might be the last time I get to pet him.

Sarah looks over her shoulder at me with a small smile when she reaches the podium. Lifting her chin, she addresses the crowd. "Hi, um, I'm Sarah. I know I've never spoken to most of you, but I've lived here with Fink since I was nine years old. I had a family and a real name once, but I don't remember them." Her voice breaks, and she inhales a deep breath, presumably trying to compose herself. Holding out her arm, she points to her scars. "I've been cut countless times, put through endless procedures, and raped nearly every single day. While I know this trial is for John, I think it's important you know what he was saving me from, and why he didn't want Sandy, the Mundane girl, to have the same life." Turning toward Fink, she speaks directly to him. "I will never be who I could have been because of you. You killed the child I was and cut out any chance of me having my own."

Her words click into place, and I gape at him. Ever since Ogier mentioned her infertility, I've had questions, there just hasn't been a time that felt right to broach the subject. When I found out, I had assumed it was because of natural causes, so hearing that she was forced to be barren has me wanting to cross the stage and beat the piss out of Fink's crippled ass. The only thing stopping me is the effect it could have on the trial. While I've never thought about having children before, seeing as corpses can't be knocked up, knowing it's impossible with Sarah because of Fink causes a painful ache in the center of my chest.

Facing back toward the residents, she continues, "All these things were done by a man who says he cared for me. At one time, I believed he did. Ogier didn't even like me, so you can imagine how horrendous my short time with him was. John is the first person that has ever let me decide if I want to be touched. He is the first person that really cares about my thoughts and feelings. I know he broke a lot of rules, but he did it to save me, not to hurt anyone. Please don't punish him for trying to help me." She walks away before rushing back to the podium. "Thank you."

Every single eye is on Sara as she returns to her seat. I doubt any of them have ever heard her speak more than a few words. Even Mayor Greer seems a little taken aback as he returns to the pulpit.

"Thank you for sharing, Sarah. I have known Fink my entire life, and John since he first arrived. Both men have my respect. While it's pretty clear that John did some things that are in clear violation of our laws, and Fink was well within his legal rights, I think intent should play a major part in your decision tonight. John did what he did because he fell in love and wanted to protect her. Both men are an asset to this town, and up until this incident, have lived here peacefully. Ogier being wounded was an unfortunate side effect, however, it was unintentional. Ingvar will eventually heal, and John was only acting in self-defense. If you must find him guilty of the charges, I propose a smaller punishment, such as community service or a fine." Adjusting the mic, he clears his throat. "Does anyone have any questions before the votes are cast?"

Mammoth's best friend, Kline, stands. He's wearing his normal clothes, which are still a bit clownish with the polka dots and stripes, but his voice is much deeper than it is when he's in costume. "My question is for John. What's keeping the girl you returned from telling the Mundaners about where she was?"

Even though I expected this question, I'm nervous that my response won't give the comfort required to ease their worry. "She just wanted to go back home. I told her she could hurt a lot of people if she mentioned where she'd been. She swore to me she wouldn't. I suppose I'm asking you to trust me."

Cyrus Klopper raises his hand. "I have a question for John as well." I don't know much about Cyrus other than he only has one eye and has a pension for wearing skin suits like the one he has on now. "What if Fink finds another kid? Will you do this again?"

I have thought about this, and honestly planned to talk to the Mayor about forbidding Mundane minors from being brought inside the gates. "I hope that doesn't happen because I don't believe a child's life should be taken from them. So, while I wouldn't go about it the same way, I would continue to fight it until the child was returned, yes." I can almost feel Fink's eyes burning holes into the side of my face. "Even if I didn't have personal issues with kidnapping children, it's dangerous for all of us. Mundane police forces are finding new and more precise ways to find evidence every day. If they come here looking for a missing child, there will be no way to stop them, and you know what happens to all of us if that occurs."

Mayor Greer waits a few seconds before

asking, "Are there any more questions?" When nobody responds, he says, "All right then. Please fill out your ballots and leave them with Officer Baron or Officer Lestar on your way out. If you would like to stay for the ruling, you are more than welcome to. Thank you for coming and doing your part to keep our town the great place that it is."

I watch as one by one, they drop their ballots into the cardboard boxes being held by Officers Baron and Lestar. I'd like to think that after hearing Sarah's, Mayor Greer's, and my testimony the residents are leaving here feeling differently than they did when they arrived. Truthfully, though, I have no idea what's going through their minds. Mayor Greer walks over to take a seat at a long folding table on the right side of the stage.

When the last form is slipped into the boxes, Officer Baron and Officer Lestar carry them to the Mayor.

Fink stands, limping off the stage as he tells him, "I need to get back to Ogier and Ingvar. I've been gone much too long already."

Mayor Greer nods. "Of course. I'll phone

you with the results."

I stand and pace back and forth to pass the time. As Mayor Greer counts and tallies the responses, Sarah climbs onto the stage, pulling me into my chair as she takes the seat next to me.

"Are you okay?" she whispers.

I take her hand, lacing our fingers together. "We're going to find out soon."

Low conversations are being held all across the room. More than half of the spectators stayed to hear the outcome, and I'm sure Fink would have remained if he didn't have to keep a close eye on Ogier. One hand holding Sarah's and the other on Nothing keeps me from going crazy while waiting. There couldn't be more than seventy votes to be counted, so Greer's got to be getting close.

Sarah's head rests on my shoulder as she takes a deep breath. "Thank you for what you said tonight. It meant a lot to hear."

Holding her chin, I give her a kiss while I know I still can. "I should have said it much sooner."

Mayor Greer's chair scrapes against the floor

as he stands and returns to the stage with his notepad. "Okay, we'll start with the lowest votes and go from there." Sarah squeezes my hand as Nothing looks up at me, apparently sensing the tension so I scratch his ear. "Banishment from Hallows Grove came in with only two votes." It's not too surprising, banishing someone risks them telling the wrong people about the kind of town this is. "Death by dismemberment or hanging has also been eliminated with ten votes." A small sob escapes from Sarah before she hurries to cover her mouth. When she turns to look at me, her eyes are wet with tears. She moves her hand, and I see she's smiling before her arms squeeze around my neck in a tight hug. It's still so foreign to have someone care this much about me. "Innocence also is off the table coming in at twelve votes." Fuck. I wish he would just say it already instead of putting on this show of his. "With eighteen votes, there will be no jail time."

I let out a huge breath, leaning forward on my knees. "Oh, thank God."

"Which means Johnathan Tarik Skelver will serve no less than a thousand hours of community service or pay no less than a five thousand dollar fine for his crimes." There are a few claps across the room before they are dismissed. "Again, thank you for your participation. I hope you all have a good evening."

I stand and Sarah jumps up after me. "What does that mean exactly?"

Pulling her against my chest, I laugh, relieved that I'm not being locked in a cell or worse. "It means I'll be doing a lot of free labor for a while."

Even though I messed up, most of the town trusts me enough to give me another chance. There are of course those who believe that I deserve to die for what I did, but Fink was bound to have some people take his side.

Mayor Greer walks up to us with clasped hands. "Congratulations, John." He nods to Sarah. "You did a fantastic job tonight."

Her skin turns pink as she smiles. "Thank you."

"Can I have a minute with John?"

Sarah looks at me, and I nod in the direction of my house. "Take Nothing home. I'll be there in a bit." Even saying that gives me chills. From the grin on her face, I'd be willing to bet she likes hearing it just as much.

Waiting until she's out of earshot, Mayor Greer says, "You made a good point tonight about the unwanted attention that allowing Mundane minors inside the gates could potentially bring. I'd like you to write up a proposition for me to present to the council."

I can feel myself gaping at him. Is he serious? "Really? That would be incredible." He can be a prick, there's no denying that, but right now I could hug him. "Thank you...I don't know what to say."

"Don't get mushy. No offense, but this isn't about your feelings. This is about protecting Hallows Grove." He tucks his hands into his pockets, backing away from me. "Bring the proposition to my office on Monday when we go over where you need to be for this week's service hours. Now go home and fuck the girl you just risked everything for." He chuckles to himself on his way off the stage.

While I plan on doing just that, right now, I'm more excited to tell her about the proposition. If it gets passed by the town council, then nothing

like what Fink did to Sarah and Sandy will ever
happen again.

ORIGINS
Sarah Stein

December 14th ~ Evening

I STILL CAN'T BELIEVE THIS IS REALLY MY LIFE. Nothing snores loudly, curled up next to me on the couch. John's in the kitchen, singing along to Christmas music as he cooks dinner. The smile that never seems to go away sprawls across my face.

John's obsession with celebrating Christmas has been getting crazier. The inside of the house has become completely unrecognizable. Every time we go into the Mundane World, we come back with more ornaments, tinsel, or Christmas lights. Every single taxidermized animal is wearing a Santa hat. John even bought Nothing the cutest red light up nose. Since I gave him a candy cane the first time he wore it, Nothing now gets excited every time we put it on him.

Christmas feels like our own special secret since nobody else around here cares about it. It does make me think of Sandy, though. I just hope she's okay.

A commercial comes on that I've seen a few times. I'm not completely sure what it's about, but I like the song so I sing along.

"I don't eat, and I don't sleep, but I got the cleanest house on the street! Oh, meth. Mmmmm meth!"

John walks into the parlor with our food, laughing. It's such a sexy sound that I swear I get wet every time I hear it. "Yeah, I don't think that commercial is having the desired effect."

He hands me a bowl full of spaghetti. It's weird that we always eat on the couch. There's a table in the kitchen, so why don't we ever use it?

"John?"

With a mouthful of food, he just answers, "Hmmm?"

"Why don't we ever eat at the dinner table?"

The question seems to catch him off guard. He swallows his bite and leans back. "I don't know. I think because my mother always made us eat at the table growing up. When I started living on my own, I took advantage of doing everything I'd never been allowed to do when I was with her."

He doesn't talk a lot about his past. I know it was painful, I just don't know many of the details. "Where is your mom?"

His fork twirls around in his bowl as he stares at the pasta. "She died of cancer when I was sixteen. I got emancipated at fifteen, so I wasn't living with her, but I wouldn't have been able to take care of her even if I had."

Esty was the only person I've ever known who's died, and that was a special kind of horrible, even though I didn't really know her. It's impossible for me to imagine what losing a mom would feel like. "That's really sad. I'm so sorry."

With a sigh, he swallows another bite. "I had a...complicated relationship with my mother." He shrugs. "Dealing with her death was equally complex."

"Why was it complicated?" I try not to ask too many questions, so I really hope I'm not annoying him right now. I just want to know everything about him, and I'm learning there's a lot.

"Let's just say Mom had some 'issues.' I think her father fucked her up in the head. I don't know much about my grandfather, but I know when my mother was a little girl, he made her undergo a genital mutilation procedure. It was the source of a lot of fights between my parents."

My mouth falls open. I had always assumed that if I had stayed with my family, my life would have been less painful. What if my real father was worse than Fink?

"Why would he do that?"

Using a napkin, John wipes spaghetti sauce from his face. "His family was from Egypt, and there, it's a fairly common practice. At least that's what I was told. Anyway, it ended up giving her a very skewed outlook on sexuality. I never met him, but what she told me about my grandfather suggested he was ruthless. My mom was always hard on me, but one night, my father hurt her...badly. He disappeared the next day and we never saw him again. She changed after that. Things got worse. She did some cruel things to me growing up that I don't think I'll ever be able to forgive her for."

I want to ask him what she did. I've told him stories about what Fink did to me, but I don't want to push him. I want him to tell me on his own.

"Do you ever think about your dad? Wonder where he is?"

He finishes his last bite before answering. "Not very often. I have zero desire to ever see him again." Standing, he kisses my head and changes the subject. "I'm gonna shower and start getting ready for tonight."

One thing I've realized the past few weeks is that I don't know John as well as I thought I did. I've always seen him as this flawless creature, but he has scars as deep as I do. The only difference is that I wear mine on the outside. Slowly, he's been revealing himself, morsel by morsel, and I greedily gobble up every bite he shares with me. I didn't think it was possible to care even more for him than I already do, yet every single day I'm proven wrong.

Nothing and I watch John while he puts on his skull makeup. It's so neat to see the transformation, even Nothing seems mesmerized by it. I try not to pout whenever John leaves. I know he has a business to run, and leaving the notes was my idea. I do understand, but he refuses to let me come with him, and he's usually gone for so long.

His smell fills my lungs as he grins at me in the mirror. "You're sulking."

"Can't I come just this once? I'll stay in the car. Please?"

He sighs as he finishes applying the setting powder. Crossing his arms, he leans against the sink. "Sarah... if I get caught and you're there, I don't know what would happen to you. I refuse to risk that."

I know he's protecting me, so I stop myself before pointing out that he's only leaving a letter, not graverobbing. It just gets so lonely here without him.

He brushes off his face, sending little powder particles into the air. "And don't say it's only a note because it's not. It's a very incriminating one."

My mouth falls open as I gape at him. Did he just read my mind? "How did you know that's what I was thinking?"

His adorable laugh sends tingles across my flesh . "We've had this conversation a few times." As he makes his way to me, he smirks, making me wish I could see his dimples. His hands squeeze my waist, pulling me tight to him. "It'll only be a couple of hours." Dropping his voice, he brings his lips close to mine. "I'll make it up to you when I get back. I promise."

The last thing I want is to make him feel guilty for trying to keep me safe, so I give him a soft kiss, careful not to smear the greasepaint as I rub his growing erection over his pants. "I'll hold you to that."

He groans. "I think I liked it better when you were pouting." I love how much he makes me laugh. It really is a whole different world, living here with him. With one last kiss to my head, he says, "I love you. I'll be back soon."

Passing me, he takes Nothing with him and leaves me alone with my thoughts. Writing the apology letters to the families of the dead girls actually seems to make him…sunnier. Though he hasn't told me as much, I think he's being choosier with the bodies he digs up as Skeleton King. With the last one, I heard him say it had to be a 'John' or 'Jane Doe.' Apparently, that means nobody knows who they are, therefore, there are no friends or family to effect.

I sigh, falling back against the couch in the parlor. Vince's *meow* sounds outside the window. He figured out I was living here at some point and now comes to see me every day. Sometimes, John lets him come inside, but Vince torments Nothing who now hides in the corner every time he's here.

Walking onto the front porch, I kneel next to my kitty and scratch my fingers across his back. I love Vince so much. I just hate that he makes me think about Fink.

Although John hasn't forbidden me from seeing him, he's made it clear he would be more comfortable if we weren't ever in the same vicinity. I truly do understand his worries, but the fact remains that Fink is the only person who can tell me where I come from. It's something that's been gnawing away bits of my brain for weeks.

After an hour of boring TV and a bath, I can't stand it anymore. I walk to the guest bedroom where John set up my sewing machine. He got it for me the first week I was here, and he's always bringing me new fabrics and patterns. I've tried, but I still don't feel comfortable in anything besides loose dresses.

I decide to wear one of my new, floral-patterned shirtdresses before applying some make-up. Putting on the cosmetics John bought me gives me more understanding as to why he gains power from his paint. Having my face made up feels like some kind of pretty armor. With a deep breath, I look in the mirror, reminding myself of the kind things John says to me every day while simultaneously trying to ignore the thoughts Fink has imbedded into my psyche all these years. After giving Vince a kiss on his tiny black head, I head down the street.

As I creep up the pathway leading up to Fink's front door, nausea unexpectedly hits me. There were so many nights I snuck up this walk, terrified about what was waiting on the other side of the door. Taking a deep breath, I reach up to ring the doorbell, the high-pitched chime chewing on my nerves.

I expect Ingvar to answer, so I'm surprised to be met with a smiling Fink and a giggling Madame Emerald when the door opens. His face falls the moment he sees that it's me.

"What are you doing here, Sarah?" he sneers.

It's odd how much his disdain for me hurts. For years, he told me how much he loved me and cared for me. Now, he can't even look at me without repulsion.

"I have some questions…ones that only you can answer."

His face falls blank and emotionless, yet his knuckles are white from how hard he's gripping his cane. "I don't have an obligation to you anymore. You made certain of that."

Madame Emerald's long fingernails trail over his arm. "Finky, darling. Answer the poor girl's questions." Her red painted lips brush against his ear. "Please?" she whispers seductively.

I've always thought Madame Emerald looked so elegant. Today she's wearing a green fur dress and her makeup is perfectly in place. I never would have put her and Fink together, but now that I see them, they look really cute. I find myself hoping for Fink's happiness. As much as I don't want to admit it, I think a part of me will always have a platonic love for him, even if I wish I didn't.

All of his resolve evaporates as he looks at her, nodding his agreement. He was never that way with me. When Madame Emerald reaches out to touch my arm, I see that she hasn't been spared from his blade. Fresh stitching wraps around her wrist that's red and healing.

"Lovely, isn't it? It's new." I look up at her, embarrassed that she caught me staring only to find her grinning with pride. She holds her hand out, spinning her arm to admire his work. "We're doing my foot next," she squeals with a wink before waving me inside. "Come in, darling. I'll bring you two some treats."

It feels uncomfortable being back here. It's weird to no longer belong in a place that was once all I knew. I follow Fink into the living room as Madame Emerald's heels *clickety-clack* across the floor. He sits on the couch, so I choose the chair on the other side of the coffee table. We stare at each other for so long the silence becomes awkward. A *crunch* sound causes me to look toward the hall where I see Ingvar peeking in, chewing on his dog biscuit. I hold my hand up in a wave to which he responds by disappearing. I wonder if he's glad I'm gone?

When Madame Emerald returns with a tray of pumpkin cookies and green juice, I feel obligated to say something.

"How did you two, um…how long have you been together?"

Madame Emerald sits next to Fink, brushing her blonde hair away from her face, revealing another wound across her forehead. "Well, after you got him into such a tizzy, you naughty girl," her hand waves at me in a playful way, "he came to see me to have his fortune read. Well, let me tell you, we were both in for quite a surprise! I've never seen myself in someone else's reading before." Her hand trails down his arm. "Our futures are intertwined." Leaning back against the couch, she crosses her legs and fondles her large, orange beaded necklace. "I've been staying here for a few weeks while Finky makes some improvements on me."

She's clearly enamored with his experimenting on her. Even though it may not make sense to me, I truly hope they make each other happy.

"Have a cookie, darling. I baked them fresh today."

I smile at her, reaching for the plate as Fink clears his throat. "You're here to ask questions, and I know they aren't about my relationship, so let's hear them."

Madame Emerald adjusts her fur hat with one hand while placing her other on Fink's arm. "Don't be rude, Finky," she says sweetly.

I'm shocked when he not only refrains from scolding her, he also sighs and softens his voice. "What would you like to know, Sarah?"

My pulse picks up in anticipation. I've dreamed about having these answers, and now I'm really going to get them.

"Where did I come from?"

Licking his lips, Fink rests his cane against the edge of the couch. "The first time I saw you was in your front yard playing with your younger brother. For a broken second in time, I thought you were *my* Sara. After that, I followed you and your family for weeks." Hot tears well up in my eyes as my skin burns around my insides. I had parents. A brother. "Your parents had a habit of leaving you in the yard by yourselves. I assume they felt a false sense of security in their quaint, little neighborhood. The music box that you love so much was what ultimately brought you to me." Madame Emerald holds up a finger, but says nothing as she gets up to leave the room. "I turned it on next to your fence, and you were immediately drawn to it, coming close within minutes. You were awestruck. All it took was me telling you that you could keep it if you came over to play with my little girl first."

Memories clash around in my mind. I remember the fence, his car…the music box. The first tingle of fear I felt when his daughter was nowhere to be found. The terror when I first heard the *click* of the lock to my new room. My family, though, I'm struggling to remember their faces.

"What was my name? My real name?"

He takes a deep breath, rubbing his forehead

as if trying to massage out the memory. When he meets my eyes, I swallow. "Timara."

Timara.

The air is knocked from my lungs when a woman's faint voice sounds in the back of my mind.

"We love you so much Timara. You're our little butterfly. Don't be scared to spread your wings."

My tears fall so hard, I gasp. Covering my face, I wipe them away and try to compose myself. There were people in my life who loved me the way a child is meant to be loved. He took that from me.

"Where?" I bite out. Getting angry at him might make him stop talking, so I force down my fury. "Where did I live?"

He waves his hand as if it doesn't matter. "A place a few hours north. Waltford, I think it was called."

Excitement has me sitting on the edge of the chair. John could take me to meet them. I wish I could remember their names.

"Do you know if they're still there?"

Straightening, he struggles against his cane to stand. "I've told you many times that I saved you, so I'm sure you've wondered what it was I saved you from." He walks to a shelf in the corner, moving a few books before taking out a square pink one. "If you would have stayed, you would be long dead."

He hands me the book, and I find it odd that there's no title. When I open it, I see the first few pages have been ripped out. There's a picture of me when I was a young child wearing a pink *My Little Pony* shirt. It's so odd that I can barely recall anything before Fink took me, but I remember adoring that shirt. The photo is fastened beneath the words: *Nine Years Old.* I turn to the next page to find a newspaper article. My eyes get wet, blurring my vision as I read the headline that destroys years of hope.

Family of Three Found Dead
Tuesday, December 13, 1983

Stephen and Delanie Burtone, along with their seven-year-old son, Trent, were found dead by a family friend Monday morning. This isn't the first time tragedy has struck the Burtone family. Last June, a missing persons report was filed for their daughter Timara (9), who was never found.

Police have ruled out foul play, determining their deaths were a result of improper exhausting of fumes in their fireplace which released carbon monoxide into the home, poisoning the family.

"They're all dead," I whisper, more to myself than to him.

I shake my head because it's so unfair. I've spent years fantasizing about reuniting with the family I lost. So many hours of dreaming, wasted.

Just then, Madame Emerald walks in, holding my music box in her hands. I want to scream at myself for how desperately I reach for it. Why does it mean so much to me? Now that I know its origins, I should despise it for sealing my fate. Regardless, I still long for the comfort it's always given me.

"Here, darling. I thought you might want this."

"Thank you." I nod, taking it from her as I stand. There's nothing else I need or want from Fink. It hasn't been that long since he let me go, so I truly hope that one day I'll be able to be in his presence without this war fighting in my soul, constantly ripping me to shreds between loving and hating him.

Looking at him now, I can't believe I let him have so much control over me. I may be broken, but broken things can be fixed. What he is, though…he's ruined. Ruined things can't ever be repaired or made into what they once were, but they can be made into something else, something new. And that? That's what I want for him.

"I'll let myself out." My words are nasally from the tears pleading to be released.

"Take the photo album too. I have no use for it any longer."

I nod, tucking the pink book under my arm and walking out the door for what I hope is the last time.

As I step off his porch, I let the tears fall. I had a family that I know in the deepest part of my heart loved me. Even though Fink stole that from me, he also brought me to the place where I met John.

What if everything happens the way it's supposed to? Without experiencing despair and torment, it might have been impossible for me to appreciate the reprieve from it all. Maybe the pain I suffered was currency to pay for the bliss my life has become?

Vince sits on the front porch when I get home. Home. The word was never more comforting than it is right now. When home was a place I was forced to be, it had a sense of suffocation, but living with John, it now represents freedom. Freedom to just be me.

I pet his back before walking inside. "Come on, Vince. Nothing isn't here, so you'll have nobody to torture."

He follows me to the parlor, curling up on my lap when I sit on the couch. I place my music box on the side table as I open the pink book. It appears to be a documentation of my life over the years. I remember Fink taking pictures, but I never really questioned why or what he did with them. Ten years of my life, in between a few pages. Aside from a ton of photos, there's a baggie with a lock of red hair and a few tiny teeth. Vince purrs next to me, rubbing his head against my thigh.

When the phone rings, I jump at the intrusive sound, causing Vince to scurry away. I let it ring a few times while I decide if I should answer, eventually giving in to my curiosity. Once I cross the kitchen, I lift the tan phone from the receiver.

"H-hello?"

"Sarah? This is Mayor Greer."

He speaks in a rushed voice and I hope whatever he needs isn't urgent. "Yes. It's me. John isn't here, though." Vince curls his body around my ankle as I lean against the counter.

The Mayor sighs into the phone. "I know, sweetheart." He's always been so nice to me, and I usually like that he calls me that. Today though, it makes me uneasy for some reason, maybe his unusual tone of voice. "John cares a lot for you, so I assume he would want me to let you know." My heart pounds harder and faster with each beat. I want to scream at him to tell me what's happening, yet I'm also absolutely terrified to hear what he has to say. "Harley, the gatekeeper, found John unconscious in his car. It looks like he's been shot."

I can barely keep my grip on the phone as my other hand clutches the edge of the counter to hold me upright. No, no, no, this isn't

THE DIRTY HEROES COLLECTION

happening. The Mayor must have gotten his wires crossed somewhere.

"Where is he?" The words come out, yet they're barely audible. My brain is shorting out like a lightbulb.

"He's with Fink. He and Ingvar are prepping him for surgery now."

Surgery.

He's alive. Like I've been given a jump-start, energy jolts through my veins. "I'm coming over there."

"No, Sarah. You don't need to—"

I'm not even sure if I got the phone hung up all the way when I run out the front door, slamming it behind me. It takes me less than three minutes, and I'm gasping for breath by the time I make it to Fink's.

Mayor Greer stands next to his and John's cars, smoking a cigarette with Nothing sitting at his feet. The sweet puppy runs to me as the Mayor meets me at the edge of the driveway. "You shouldn't have come, Sarah."

I clasp my hands together, debating if falling to my knees would be too much. "Please, just let me see him for a second. I'll be quick. I'm begging you."

He grumbles something under his breath before tossing his cigarette to the ground. "You have two fucking minutes."

He's clearly irritated that I'm here, so I run to the front door, yelling over my shoulder, "Thank you, Mayor."

Fink can't hurt me anymore, so I don't waste any time knocking. The foyer is empty as I sprint up the stairs, taking them two at a time. As soon as I cross the threshold of Fink's lab, I see John covered in blood, fastened to a table next to Ogier.

Tears burn my eyes as I cover my mouth. He isn't moving. "Oh, God."

"Sarah! What the hell are you doing here?"

Ignoring Fink's question, I hurry to stand next to John. I'm able to suppress most of my sobs, but a few of them escape when I hold his hand and feel how cold it is.

"I love you," I whisper. I try to stop crying, but that only makes me cry harder. "Please be okay. I need you."

His eyes flutter when Fink barks. "You need to get out. I'm about to operate."

"Please help him. I'll forgive you for everything if you just save him."

Even though he's upset with John, he has Madame Emerald now. Surely he won't let him die if he can save him.

He rolls his eyes. "I have no use for your forgiveness. Regardless, I do plan to do the best I can. Now, for the last time, get out." Ingvar pulls me away from John as I cry over his shoulder loud enough that hopefully he can hear me.

"I promised you I wouldn't ever leave you, so you aren't allowed to leave me either!"

With tears blurring my vision, I'm dragged down the stairs where Madame Emerald squeals, "Oh hello again, Sarah darling!" just as Ingvar shoves me toward the entryway.

"Sarah go away," is the last thing I hear before the door is slammed in my face.

MEANT TO BE
John Skelver

December 15th ~ Morning

NOTHING SNIFFS THE SNOW COVERING THE dead girl's empty grave as I lay the note on top of the tombstone. Her name was Kate. She hadn't been embalmed when she was buried, allowing me to taxidermize her. She'd been a beautiful brunette with a tribal band tattoo around her ankle. It seems so long ago now, my time with the dead. Sarah has completely consumed my entire life, making it more than I could had ever come close to imagining.

Every time I do this, it feels like a kink gets loosened. For so long I'd forced myself to reject any emotion that made me uncomfortable. While I still struggle, I do my best to really *feel*. Whether it's guilt, embarrassment, or uselessness, I push myself through the discomfort to try to understand the emotion and do what I need to do to make amends.

Nothing sticks his tail straight up, barking in a frenzy when the sound of a gun *cocking* behind me causes my body to freeze mid-movement.

"You're the one that took my sister, aren't you?"

I hold my hands up, cautiously turning around to find a boy that couldn't be much older than thirteen or fourteen pointing a shaky handgun at my chest. His eyes narrow, fear flashing across his features the moment he sees my face paint. It's nearly one o'clock in the morning. It's odd that, as I stare down the barrel of the gun, I wonder how worried his parents are about him.

With careful movements, I take a small step, shushing Nothing who's growling next to me. "I am."

"I heard my parents talking about all the notes you've been leaving. They thought you'd come here eventually. What did you need her body for?" If I can get the gun out of his hand, maybe I can talk him down and give him some sort of closure, but I can't think clearly with the barrel pointed at my chest. The snow *crunches* as I try to close in on him. "Don't get any closer to me, or I'll shoot you in your face."

"I didn't intend to hurt your family." I lean forward, slowly attempting to move my foot. "I'm trying to—"

Bang!

The impact of being hit doesn't hurt immediately. My mouth falls open as I watch the blood slowly seeping across my white T-shirt. Holding my side, I push down to add pressure while the boy watches me in shock. As if suddenly realizing what he's done, he drops the gun and runs from the cemetery.

"Fuck," I murmur.

Warm liquid wets my fingers, and I drop to my knees, burning heat flaming up my side. Shit. How am I going to get back to town? I'm maybe half an hour away. I don't know if I can drive that far. "Goddamn it!" I groan as Nothing whines next to me. "It's okay, boy. Let's just get back to the car."

Considering I barely make it the short walk to my Buick, I have no idea how I'm going to make it home. Getting into the car doesn't ease my discomfort, but it's a relief to not have to keep walking.

At first, I think I might make it, but then the pain becomes too much and my vision distorts with black spots. For the first time, I'm terrified that I'm dying. My life feels like it just started with Sarah. Simply thinking of her has me pushing harder on the gas pedal. I refuse to die without seeing her one last time.

Nothing continues barking as if he's trying to keep me awake. It works for most of the drive until the car rumbles from the car drifting over sleeper lines. Relief almost makes me pass out again when the south gate comes into view.

Not only is it a miracle that I didn't get pulled over, I can't believe I actually made it to the gate. As I reach out to enter the code, darkness folds over me, and I'm consumed with the sensation of falling.

The last thing I feel is Nothing's tongue licking my arm as he whimpers next to me.

THE DIRTY HEROES COLLECTION

* * *

"I love you." It's her. Her tearful voice softly pleads, "Please be okay. I need you." While I can't open my eyes or speak, her name is on repeat in my mind. *Sarah. Sarah. Sarah.*

I feel my favorite sensation. Her heat. I can feel her hand squeezing mine as Fink reprimands her. I wish I could make my voice work so I could tell her to get away from him. If I could just open my eyes.

Though I can't follow everything they're saying, I hear her begging Fink to save me, forcing my memory to replay in flashing images.

The graveyard.

The letter.

The little boy.

The gun.

The black is closing in again. Her heat disappears. Why can't I open my eyes? I just want to see her...one more time. As my body falls back into the abyss, she screams into the darkness.

"I promised you I wouldn't ever leave you, so you aren't allowed to leave me either!"

December 25th ~ Morning

JESUS. IF I HAVE TO SPEND ONE MORE SECOND IN this fucking lab, my brain is going to explode. It's been a week and a half of mostly bedrest. Since my surgery, Sarah's only been allowed to visit three times. I miss her terribly, and over the last few days, I've been missing her in more ways than one.

I've felt considerably better, and my libido has returned back to its original state. I won't be able to actually fuck her for another week or so, but there's plenty more we can do until then. And not to mention, I miss the shit out of Nothing. Sarah brought him each time she visited, which ended up only making me miss him more.

Fink continues to rattle off all the self-care requirements for healing at home, even though he's already been over this twice before.

"Yeah, I get it. Can I please go now?"

He tilts his head in a chiding way as Ingvar

hands me a bottle of pills. "You don't know how lucky you are, my boy. That bullet went clean through and was less than half an inch from your large intestine. The unlikeliness of that is astounding. And we still need to keep an eye out for blood clots. Swing by next week so I can look you over. In the meantime, have Sarah page me if you have any nausea or vomiting, bloody stool, d—"

"Really, Fink, I know what I'm supposed to do. I'm just ready to go."

He taps his cane against the floor and nods. "Fair enough." Pointing to the bottle in my hand, he adds, "Take those twice a day with food. Believe me, they're better than anything you could find at the apothecary." He gestures to the door. "Mayor Greer will be here soon to take you home."

I get off the bed, stifling a yell when a sharp pain lights up my right side. Fink said I'd be sore for a bit, but I'm not about to risk him keeping me here for a minute longer.

"Thanks, Fink...for saving my life."

He simply nods with a grunt.

I don't necessarily think he's forgiven me

for what happened with Sarah and Sandy or that I unintentionally killed Ogier, however I do know how much he respects the laws of this town. He told me himself that my trial was fair.

Considering we have to live peacefully in town together, I'm also trying to tolerate him and just move on, but I still don't want Sarah around him. I will say, since he's been with Madame Emerald, he's been slightly more... sane.

Speaking of the kind woman, she greets me at the bottom of the stairs with a tin full of what I'm assuming are her cookies. She apparently loves to bake as much as tell fortunes. I think I might have gained five pounds in the ten days I've been here.

"Here you go, darling. Take these with you to keep your energy up. This town needs their Skeleton King."

I smile. "Thank you—"

The doorbell cuts me off, and she hurries to answer it, revealing Mayor Greer. Greeting Madame Emerald, he says "Good morning," before he sets his sights on me, nearly barreling over her without waiting for an invitation.

"John! It's so wonderful to see you walking amongst the living! Are you ready to go?"

"You have no idea."

I pass him and he turns on his heel to follow me outside. Once we're in the car and backing out of Fink's driveway, Mayor Greer hands me a brown paper bag. "Here, I got what you asked for." My stomach switches places with my heart as I look inside. "I'm glad you're on the upswing for more than one reason. Your proposition has actually been received better than I foresaw."

My head snaps up to grin at him. "Seriously?"

"Well yes, however, the council has some questions they like to ask before they proceed, so I scheduled a meeting tonight."

I gape at him. I was literally just shot. "But it's Christmas."

He looks at me like I grew another face. "So?"

"I have plans with Sarah."

"It won't take that long. Just a few clarifications. I'll pick you up at seven."

Since I obviously don't have a choice, there's no point in arguing. "Fine."

He hasn't even pulled into my driveway yet when Sarah and Nothing run across the snow-covered yard to greet me. Tucking the paper bag into my jacket, I step out of the car where Sarah wraps me in a hug so tight, I flinch from the stab of pain.

She immediately lets me go. "Sorry."

I bend down to pet Nothing before wrapping my arm around her waist, waving to Mayor Greer as we walk inside.

The moment the door opens, I laugh at the transformation of my living room. She's been busy. The tree is completely decked out. Stockings hang from the fireplace and garland is wrapped around the spiral bannister. Christmas lights are strung up from the ceiling while the Santa figurine and snow globe collections have only grown.

I'm a little nervous to look at the bill for the credit card I got her, but the way she holds her hands up and spins in a circle, clearly proud of the work she's done, makes any debt she may have accumulated completely worth it. "Merry Christmas!"

Pulling her against me, I revel in her

warmth, which I've missed terribly, kissing her hard. "Merry Christmas, Sarah."

Backing away from me, she takes my hand to lead me into the parlor. "I got you a Christmas present…but I got bored and asked Eunice to help me set it up. I've been playing it for a few days. You died of dysentery, and a thief stole all my oxen, so I'm stuck."

My laugh bubbles up my throat. I have no idea what that means. "What?"

As soon as we cross the threshold of the parlor, I see it. She got me a computer. Excitement pushes up my smile. I've talked about wanting one, so knowing that she really listened to me and made the effort to get it pushes a comforting buzz through my entire body.

"No way." I rush over to it, hurrying to turn on the modem.

"Mayor Greer helped me get it. He even put internet on it!" Her hands clasp together before leaning over to pull out a floppy disk. "And this is the best part. It's a game. You have to make it to Oregon with everyone in the wagon. It's really hard."

She shows me how to play before leaving me

to navigate the internet. The moment she walks out, I reach into my jacket to take out the paper bag. Once I empty it, I throw the bag away and shove its contents into the pocket of my coat before sitting back at the computer. The shrill sound of the dial-up has me tapping my fingers on the desk in anticipation. I've heard about chat rooms being a hotbed for any information ever imagined, so I start there.

I'm still fiddling with my fabulous gift until the smell of something sweet floats into my nostrils.

"Pie is ready!" Sarah calls from the kitchen.

For some reason, I'm overcome with the urge to laugh. Never in a million years would I have thought this could be my life.

December 25th ~ Day

Sarah has the whole day planned. Eggnog and pie with a corny Christmas movie about a little boy whose family somehow forgot him when they went on vacation, leaving him to fend for himself against a couple of horribly idiotic robbers. Sarah finds it amusing, if her sweet giggling is any indication.

Her head is in my lap as the credits roll, and with the proximity of her mouth next to my cock, my hard-on begins to grow. She must feel it against her cheek because she lifts up to look at me with a sexy grin. Her fingers slowly lower my sweats. When my erection pops free, she licks it from base to tip.

I watch her, holding her hair in a ponytail to allow me to fully see her face. While of course this feels epic, for some reason, it's my heart that's currently being affected most. She's so fucking beautiful and kind, smart and forgiving. I truly don't deserve her, and I won't let a day pass without praying she never figures that out.

God, I wish I could feel more than her mouth. I love watching the way her body moves while pleasuring me. It's so fucking difficult to not thrust between her lips, but I can't risk delaying my healing time. Regardless, with her hot tongue against my dick, it doesn't take more than a few minutes for every cell in my body to spark to life as my come spurts down her throat.

"I love you so fucking much," I moan through the pleasure. And it's true. She's the only one for me, and I'll die happy if it stays that way.

She sits up on her knees, cupping my cheek as she whispers, "I love you too," between kisses.

Lying back on the couch, I point to her dress. "Take that off and get over here."

What she's wearing now is a new one that she's sewn herself, red and green for today's occasion. She pulls it over her head without hesitation, revealing her nude form in front of me. The sight of her pussy makes my heart bang around in my chest which only increases when she hovers over my mouth and begs for my tongue. I lap at her clit, loving the way she rocks against my mouth.

Her movements are doing most of the work, so my fingers find her hole to bring her closer. "I've touched myself every night thinking of this."

Her confession has me sucking her hard, little nub into my mouth. Knowing that I was in her thoughts so frequently heats up my flesh as

I lap and lick like I'll never taste her again.

When she finds her release, she gives me what I've been craving, leaving both me and the couch drenched in her fluids.

Once her breathing calms some, she looks down at me, running her fingers through my hair. "I was so scared."

It kills me for her to be anything besides happy. "I'm fine, Sarah. I just got you, and I'm not going anywhere."

Shifting her body down, careful to not put any weight on my wound, she lies next to me, snickering. "You're soaking wet."

I laugh at the mild embarrassment she still experiences. She knows I love it, though. "Let's go take a shower. I need to get ready for the council meeting tonight."

She leans up on her shoulder with furrowed brows. "Tonight? But it's Christmas!"

"You know we're the only ones that care about that. At least the Mayor promised it won't last long."

Her eyes squint playfully as she gets off the couch. "Ugh. Fine. You owe me one."

She heads down the hall to the bathroom,

not waiting for me to follow. "I think I can handle that." I laugh, rushing as quickly as I'm able to meet up with her.

After we're clean, she leaves me to get ready. It's been so long since I've worn my skull paint. I decide to put it on for comfort's sake. It isn't long before Nothing takes his place on the rug, watching me. The best part, though, is that Sarah's right behind him, leaning against the door frame watching too

"I'm so glad you're finally back. I just hate that you have to leave again." I look in the mirror to see the reflection of her pouty face.

"You can come if you want, but I can't promise it won't be boring."

The glow that brightens her face shines with her grin. "It won't be boring if I'm with you."

December 25th ~ Evening

THE MEETING GOES FAIRLY SMOOTH ASIDE FROM a few mild disagreements, and by the end, it's unanimous that no Mundaner under the age of seventeen is to be allowed entrance into Hallows Grove under any circumstances.

Sarah holds my hand the entire time, jumping up the moment all documents have been signed, excited to finish our evening.

As we step outside, she zips up her coat before throwing her hands up and giggling at the snow falling in the moonlight. Nothing snaps at a few snowflakes before taking off toward the cemetery. She laces our fingers together, resting her head on my shoulder. "Can we take a walk through the cemetery? I want to give Esty her Christmas present."

I press my lips to the top of her head. "I'd like that."

Esty's plot sits on the tallest hill, giving us a beautiful view of the rest of the graveyard. Sarah pulls a small box out of her pocket, telling the headstone, "Merry Christmas, Esty. I got you something." Unwrapping it, she lays a snowflake necklace across the granite. "I hope you like it."

My heart's booming in my chest, yet somehow, I keep my voice even. "Thank you." The fear of her turning me away has mostly dissolved. I trust her completely. That doesn't mean I don't still feel like I'm going to throw up from frazzled nerves.

Her head tilts with her quizzical expression as she faces me. "For what?"

I shrug and laugh because the words sound so much less profound than they are. "For loving me."

Softening her voice, she smiles. "John…"

Taking her hand, I bring her fingers to my lips. "You've become my dearest friend, but you're more than that…" I reach into my pocket, pulling out the ring I had the Mayor get for me and slide it onto her ring finger. "You're it for me. I truly believe that. You and I were meant to be." She gasps as her tattered breath expels little white clouds from her lips. "Will you marry me, Sarah?"

Her eyes widen, showing them shiny with tears as she hugs my neck so hard, I hiss in pain. "Oh, sorry, I—I, yes! Of course," she laughs, "Absolutely yes!"

There's never been a single moment I've ever experienced that's made me feel this… drunk on bliss. We smile against each other's

lips at the promise we just made to each other.
It's me and her. John and Sarah. Forever.

EPILOGUE
John Skelver

April 3rd, 1994 ~ Afternoon

"STOP IT." SARAH SCOLDS THE SANITY Eaters. "I have to hide the eggs before you can eat the candy." She grabs the bag of plastic eggs off the picnic table to hold them behind her back.

Bolt wrinkles his nose. "Well."

Crossing his arms, Cask scoffs. "That's."

"Stupid." Jolt finishes with a roll of her eyes.

"Maybe, but it's my Easter party, and I want to do an egg hunt, so you'll just have to be patient," Sarah says in a sing-song voice.

My yard is full of people and covered in pastel decorations. I can't believe I let her talk me into this, and even more so, I'm shocked at how many people accepted her invitation. This town's never been much for 'get togethers' outside of the Halloween Games.

Nothing seems to be having a blast, playing fetch with a few of the kids waiting for the Easter egg hunt to start. Hot dogs and burgers are cooking on the grills that Kline and Mammoth insisted on bringing.

The Sanity Eaters run away from Sarah to sit with the Zeldamine sisters who are constantly coddling them. Since Ogier was the Zeldamine sister's brother-in-law, they got custody of the kids when Ogier died. I don't know if the sisters ever told them that I was the one responsible for shooting their father. If they did, the triplets have given me no indication that they're angry at me for it.

Sarah passes me to go to the refreshment table, grinning as I reach out to pull her against me, pressing my lips to hers. "Your party turned out great." She blushes, giggling when I smack her ass.

"Hello there!" Madame Emerald's voice carries across my yard, and we turn to see her waving at us with the arm that isn't looped around Fink's.

Holding up a hand in greeting, I ask Sarah through a forced smile. "You invited them?"

"I invited everyone," she whispers. "I couldn't leave them out."

As they get closer, Madam Emerald places a hand on her stomach before saying, "This looks absolutely lovely, darling! And what a perfect day for it too!" She isn't wrong about that. The sun shines bright in the blue sky as a gentle breeze blows across the newly blooming flowers. "I'm sorry Ingvar couldn't be here. He's feeling a little under the weather today."

"Thank you. And I hope Ingvar gets better soon." Sarah beams before her eyebrows narrow at Madame Emerald's hand still on her stomach. "Are you feeling all right?"

Madame Emerald giggles, and even Fink has to fight a grin. "Well...we haven't actually told anyone yet, but...we're pregnant!" she squeals.

Sarah's face completely falls as her eyes cut

to Fink's. "A baby?" Her voice is barely above a whisper. Forcing her expression into a fake smile, she's able to muster up some enthusiasm. "That's wonderful. Congratulations...to you both." Looking toward the Sanity Eaters ravishing the sweets table, she tucks a strand of hair behind her ear. "I'm sorry, will you excuse me?"

She doesn't wait for a response as she storms past the triplets to go inside. I follow behind her to find her fists balled up as she paces in the kitchen.

"Are you okay?"

Finally, she stops, looking up at me with wet eyelashes. "It's not fair! He—" She throws her hand toward the yard. "He stole any chance of us ever having kids of our own, yet *he* gets to have a baby?!"

She's been hinting about how much this bothers her more and more the past few weeks. She watches baby commercials with this defeated expression, and no matter what I say seems to make her feel better.

Her body shudders as I wrap my arms around her. "I hate him for it too, Sarah," I murmur against her temple.

"Doesn't it bother you that you'll never get to be a dad?" she sobs against my chest.

Holding her chin to lift her sorrowful gaze to mine, I shake my head. "Not as long as you're my wife." A small smile breaks through, and I capitalize on it. "Don't let that asshole ruin your Easter. Just ignore him and Madame Emerald and have fun at your party."

She sighs, hugging me again as she rests her head on my chest. "Okay. You're right."

"Besides, I think the Sanity Eaters are going to destroy our yard if you don't hide those eggs soon."

That gets me another small smile. Wiping her tears, she stands up straight, brushes off her dress, and walks back outside. I light up a joint, just about to follow her, when the phone rings behind me. Picking up the receiver, I take a drag.

"Hello?" I cough out.

"Hey, Skeleton King, this is Harley. Sorry to bother you, but Mayor Greer wants you at the south gates immediately."

I roll my eyes and groan. "May I ask why?" Greer knew we had this party today. Everyone did.

"There's uh, a Mundane man and a little kid asking for you." The gatekeeper's voice sounds as though he's not sure he should be telling me this.

My stomach threatens to eject the six deviled eggs I had earlier. This must have something to do with a body I've taken. I've been so careful, though. Every body I've taken in the past five months didn't have any known relatives. "Did they say what they want?"

"No, but please hurry."

My palms are so sweaty, I nearly drop the phone when I hang it up. Surely if this has anything to do with my graverobbing then the Mundane police would be here too? I can't think of what else it could be about. My address isn't connected to my taxidermy business, so anyone wanting to hire me would do so by calling.

I don't want to worry Sarah until I know what this is about, so I sneak out the front door, praying she doesn't hear the car starting. Hopefully I can make it back before she even notices I left. My fingers tap the steering wheel as my organs tangle in my gut. I have a weird feeling about this.

When I reach the gates, I can see a man with a little girl, but from this distance, they don't look at all familiar. Mayor Greer and Harley step out of the gate technician building to greet me as I shut my car door.

"You want to tell me why you have Mundane visitors, John?" Mayor Greer growls under his breath.

I swallow, shaking my head. "I have no idea who they are."

"That's funny," Greer snaps, "considering the man claims to have the same last name as you."

My head jerks toward the gate, sure I just misheard him. "What?" I try to make out their faces when his next words melt my shoes to the concrete.

"He says his name is Gerald Skelver."

The only parts of my body currently working are my eyes as they ping pong back and forth between the Mayor and Harley.

"No." I shake my head back and forth because there's no way that could really be my father standing just a few feet away from me.

"Either you can deal with this or I can." Mayor Greer's patience seems to be wearing thin.

"Open the gates, I'll go talk to them."

Harley nods and Mayor Greer follows him as I get back into my car. The gates open and as soon as my Buick is all the way through, they close behind me. I stare straight ahead, refusing to look at the man and child before I have to. Once I'm a few yards past the gate, I let the car idle a couple moments before turning it off. With a deep breath and a prayer that this isn't the man who abandoned me over twenty years ago, I get out of the car. This has to be some sort of mix-up.

I don't even get my car door closed when the man says, "Oh my God, Johnathan...is that really you?"

I force myself to lift my head, and I come face to face with the man who left me alone to suffer with the only broken parent I had left.

"What do you want?"

My voice comes out harsher and colder than I prefer, but he disregards it. "There's a café I saw a few miles from here. My treat if you'd like to join us"

"And why the fuck would I want to do that?"

The man who is undoubtedly my father rubs the back of his neck. "Because I need your help."

I scoff, flabbergasted by his audacity. "That's rich."

"Please, just hear me out. If you still want nothing to do with either of us afterward, we'll both understand."

The little girl holding his hand, flutters her eyes up to me. There's something in them that makes it impossible for me to walk away. "Fine. I'll give you thirty minutes. After that, I don't ever want to see you again."

"Thirty minutes is all I need," the man who I used to call 'Dad' says.

He gives me the address for the café, and I get in my car to follow him in his truck the three miles to our destination. My thoughts twist around themselves. Why is he here? Who is the little girl? How did he find me?

The small but clean café is one I've never visited before. I step over to the table they've chosen and take my seat, wishing the waitress would come take our order to dampen the awkward tension.

"How've you been?" he asks.

Crossing my arms, I lean back in the booth. "If you were concerned about my well-being, I think you would have shown up at some point in the past twenty years. At least when Mom died."

He wipes his hand across his mouth, looking into the empty space above my head. "You have every right to hate me."

"No shit," I deadpan. "How did you even find me?"

"You're in the phonebook." He shrugs and looks up to the young blonde woman in a blue uniform who's arrived to take our order. Once she walks away, he continues, "I'm not making excuses for what I did to you and your mother. I'm a recovering alcoholic, and I regret many of the things I did during my years of addiction."

I glance at my watch, avoiding the little girl's stare burning into my skull. "You might want to get to the fucking point."

With a heavy sigh, he looks down to the

child. "I'm dying. My liver's shutting down, and I don't know how much time I have left." The straining of my insides at his words doesn't make sense. He's barely been in my life at all, and the small part he was involved in, he just made worse. So why is this making my heart beat in panic? His arm wraps around the dark-haired girl before he meets my eyes. "This is your little sister, Christy."

It's as if a steel ball crashes into my ribcage. This is a lot to process, and I feel like I'm about to overload. A sister? The fact that he went on to have another child bothers me more than it should. She doesn't even look like me. She's pale like my father, and her eyes are the same green as his. Her long eyelashes flutter as she blinks at me, making me sigh. Regardless of the grudges I hold against my father, it's not this kid's fault. Lifting my hand in a wave, I smile at her.

"Hi, Christy. I'm John."

"Are you going to adopt me?" she squeaks.

My eyeballs pull against their sockets as I gape at my father who rubs his forehead with an irritated chuckle. "I was getting to that."

I can't do more than scoff as my esophagus

swells in my throat. This has to be a joke. Like an episode of Candid Camera. "You can't be fucking serious. Where's her mom?" Christy's lip quivers, making me feel like shit for my reaction.

My dad, *Gerald*, rests his forearms on the table, giving me a flashback of my mother yelling at him for doing that. "She was…sick. She…"

"Threw herself off a bridge," Christy finishes bluntly.

Now I really feel like a prick.

Our waitress drops off our drinks, and I guzzle half my coffee, wishing it was something much stronger. "I'm going to be honest with you, son." My skin prickles in gooseflesh at hearing him call me that again. "You seem like you're doing well. You have your taxidermy business, you live in that fancy gated community." I nearly choke on my drink. Hallows Grove is hardly fancy, but sure, I'll let him think that. He gestures to my ring finger. "And it looks like you have a little wife too."

Just the mention of Sarah makes me smile. I look down at the solid black, onyx band she picked out at the jewelry shop. "Her name is Sarah," I say, though, not necessarily to him.

"I don't have any other living relatives, and there's nobody in Christy's mother's family that's a viable option."

"None of them wanted me," Christy says matter-of-factly before she sucks on the straw in her milkshake.

Gerald releases an embarrassed chuckle. "She's a very honest child." The ice in his soda clinks against his glass as he takes a drink. "It's getting to the point where it's difficult to take care of myself much less her, and I'd prefer that she stays out of the foster system."

I rub the back of my neck because I have no idea how to respond. What kind of soulless jerk could say no to this? On the other hand, it's not just me or the child this decision would be affecting.

"I would need to talk to my wife before I can give you an answer."

He nods in desperation. "Oh, of course. I understand that." He and Christy look at each other, and I wonder if he ever gazed at me with that much adoration. "What if she just stayed the night tonight? Then maybe next week, we do a weekend? We can work our way up so it's not such a big shock for any of us."

Lacing my fingers, I turn to Christy. "Is this what you want?"

She blinks back tears as she nods. "I don't want to make my dad worse because he's taking care of me. And I don't want to go to an orphanage, so yes, please. I would like you to adopt me."

Jesus, this is heavy. It takes more effort than normal to exhale a deep breath. "Okay then, we can try tonight." Looking at my watch tells me I've been here way too long for Sarah to not have noticed that I left. I glance over to my father. "Hallows Grove has strict rules about visitors. You won't be given access past the gates. Are you comfortable with that?"

His smile reads something akin to pride. "As long as you'd be willing to bring her by my house on occasion?"

I sigh with my nod. "Of course."

He reaches across the table, placing a hand on my arm. "I don't deserve this kindness, but for Christy's sake, I am eternally grateful."

He pays the bill, and as we walk out to the parking lot, we make plans to meet here tomorrow afternoon so I can bring her back. Opening the cab door of his truck, he pulls out a pink Barbie suitcase.

It's awkward to stand here watching her cry while they say their goodbyes. He assures her he'll see her tomorrow, and after thanking me one last time, he climbs in his truck.

Christy rocks back on the heels of her white tennis shoes. "Can I ride in the front seat?"

I smirk at her. "Sure, kid."

She hands me her suitcase, and I put it in the trunk as she asks, "What's the shovel for?"

"Digging. Now come on, let's go."

What the hell am I doing? How is this supposed to work? I can't hide my business from her, and I can't have her talking about anything she might see. Not to mention, Mayor Greer is going to freak out. We literally just passed the law about Mundane minors three months ago. However, there won't be anyone looking for her, and if Sarah and I adopt her, she'll legally be our child and therefore a Hallows Grove resident.

We get into the car where she immediately

begins changing the radio stations. "How old are you anyway? When my dad said you were my brother, I thought you'd be..." she trails off, and I'm surprised at myself when I laugh at her trying to not offend me.

"Younger?" she smiles sheepishly. "I'm twenty-eight, which believe it or not, isn't that old." I tease her. "So, how old are you?"

"Eight and three quarters."

I'm surprised at how easy she is to be around. I thought this would be incredibly uncomfortable, yet before I know it, we're pulling up to the south gates. Even though I feel that I should warn her about the type of town this is, I honestly don't even know where to start, so I stay silent.

Holding my finger on the intercom button, I call for Harley. "Hey, it's John. Will you send for Mayor Greer? I need to speak with him."

"Never left, I'm coming out." Greer's voice crackles through the speaker.

Once he walks out of the gate technician building, I climb out of my car, telling Christy, "Stay here."

"What was all that about?" Greer barks as

he approaches me.

I drop my shoulders with a sigh, there's no easy way to say this. "That was my father. He's sick and needs me to take care of my sister... permanently."

With flaring nostrils, he looks over my shoulder. "You would have legal custody of her?" I'm surprised at how well he's taking this.

"Yes," I quickly answer, "if that's what Sarah and I decide to do."

"Sometimes, I think you're more trouble than you're worth." He's only halfway serious...I think. "Until she's officially a resident, just be careful what you let her see. And as soon as you and Sarah make your decision, bring the child to me."

"Of course, Mayor."

I'm grateful that went so much smoother than expected, and I can only hope for the same with Sarah. I get back in the car, smiling at Christy. "Are you ready?" Nodding, she looks out her window as we drive through the gates. "Welcome to Hallows Grove."

"Do you think your wife will like me?"

"Sarah's the kindest person you'll ever

meet. You really don't need to worry about her."

Just as I pull into my driveway, Sarah walks around from the backyard with her hands on her hips, looking adorably frustrated. I step out of the car, hearing the sounds of the party going on out back.

"Where did you go?" she asks, just before her eyes land on Christy climbing out of the Buick.

"It's quite the story," I say with a dry laugh. That's putting it mildly. Dropping my voice, I tell her, "We're going to need to have a discussion later." Suddenly, a small hand wraps around mine, and I look down to see Christy's fingers clutching tightly.

Sarah's mouth is gaping while her eyebrows scrunch in uncertainty. Bending over to touch her knees, she greets Christy softly, "Hello. My name is Sarah, what's yours?"

Christy's eyes scan over Sarah's scars, and I'm wondering if I should have prepared her for them. "Christy Skelver." Sarah's eyes widen as they lift up to me. "I'm Johnathan's half-sister."

Snapping up to standing, Sarah frowns. I still struggle to know how to handle her emotions sometimes. "*Johnathan* never told me he had a sister."

My eyebrows shoot up at her attitude and the way she says my full name. She's never once called me that. I can only assume the hurt in her expression is from her thinking I've kept things from her.

"*Johnathan,*" I mimic her tone, "didn't know." Her head tilts in confusion, so I'm about to elaborate when Christy beats me to it.

"Our dad is sick, and there's nobody else to take care of me."

I was kind of hoping to bring up the subject a bit more gently. All emotion is wiped from Sarah's face until a small smile begins to peek out. "Oh…I see."

Pointing behind the house, I tell Christy, "There are some kids in the backyard, why don't you go play with them? I'll bring your suitcase inside."

The very second she's out of earshot, Sarah wraps her arms around my waist. "Is she really staying with us?"

Her question comes out like a plead. I want to say yes, but we need to think this through first. Neither of us has any idea how to take care of a kid. "We'll see how things go."

"What will happen to her if we don't keep her?"

I drop my head with a sigh. I would much rather have this conversation when half the town isn't in my backyard. "She'll be put with other children that don't have anyone to look after them."

"Foster care?" She shakes her head. "John, everything I've heard about that sounds horrible."

Kissing her head, I squeeze her against my chest. "We have some time to decide. I just got you, I'm not sure if I'm ready to have our time alone together cut so short."

She nods, but I'm pretty sure in her mind, the choice has already been made.

April 3rd ~ Evening

I LEAN AGAINST THE DOORFRAME, WATCHING Sarah run her fingers through Christy's hair while she reads her a book. I'm grateful that Christy's asleep because the story is about a man who loses his mind and tries to kill his entire family. Nothing is curled up in a ball at their feet, snoring loudly.

Today went really well, and aside from a couple of issues with the Sanity Eaters being assholes, to which Sarah didn't hesitate intervening and reminding them they were guests at *her* home, Christy seemed to have a lot of fun. She was pretty much attached to Sarah's hip all evening, and Sarah definately didn't appear to mind the attention.

Grabbing a large trash bag, I go out back to try to pick up some the mess from the party. After pouring out the leftover contents in several abandoned plastic cups, I clean off one of the picnic tables.

"We have to keep her." Sarah's voice says softly. "She's supposed to be with us. I just know it."

Sitting at the table, I hold my arms out to her, to which she responds by immediately sitting on my lap. As much as I still think we should take time to really put thought into this,

I also know I'll never be able to live with myself if I turn the child away.

Sarah leans her head back against my shoulders and says in a dreamy way, "She has your nose... and dimples."

There's no logical reason why that should warm my chest as much as it does. The truth is, as confused as I am over my feelings about Christy, I know I want her to stay too. "You're completely sure about this, aren't you?"

Climbing off my lap, she lowers to her knees, slowly unzipping my pants. "One hundred percent."

Fuck, with people over here all day, we haven't been able to have sex since this morning, and we haven't gone that long since I was shot. I'm more than ready for her hot mouth, thrusting as soon as her lips wrap around me. My fingers grip her head as I push her down farther. As good as her mouth feels, it doesn't compare to her pussy.

Sliding out of her mouth, I help her to her feet before bending her over the picnic table. I hold her dress scrunched at her waist, using my free hand to yank down her panties. My fingers probe between her legs, and just as she is every time, she's soaking wet. While I slip in easily, the walls of her cunt squeeze me so tight, I groan. My God. I'm never going get used to how fucking amazing this feels. I thrust hard into her a few times, somehow getting harder at the sound of her mewling.

Gripping tight onto her hips, I continue moving myself in and out of her body. "When do you want to tell her?"

She pushes her hips back, rocking hard onto my body. "Let's surprise her." She moans. "We can…set up her…room first." Her words come out in sexy as fuck pants.

"Ewe! Are you guys doin' it?"

I've never moved so damn fast in my entire life. Sarah and I lurch away from each other as I try to shove my rock-hard cock back into my jeans. "Jesus Christ!"

"W-we, um, uh…" Sarah stutters.

I finally get halfway decent, aside from my still very prominent erection, and turn to face Christy. She's holding a blonde doll in a rainbow dress, wearing her long pink nightgown. "Are you really going to adopt me?"

Her eyes are wide with hope, and I can't help but grin. Sarah takes my hand, leading us to kneel in front of Christy. "We want nothing more." Sarah's voice reveals that she's on the verge of tears.

Christy lunges forward, wrapping her arms around both of us. "Thank you, thank you!"

Of course I'm terrified, but I was terrified with Sarah too. I have a wife I never thought I would have, and now a family I'd never even considered possible.

Maybe what Sarah says is true. Everything happens the way it's meant to.

Lights. I'm a shadow. I have no
substance. I'm the whisper behind you that
you think you heard. I'm the one that swallows
your light like a black hole. You think you see
me, but like my pop says, I'm just a puppet. A
blip. Air. A thought gone by.

I'll never be real.

But at least my life isn't real. When I'm in the
life that really pulls me is when I get to the one
thing that really feels tangible and different. It
were just a set fall. The girls, the girls... Every
body says she and the only one I ever give me
feel. She touches me in ways I can't explain me...
because I know she is all that I could be.

The urge to keep going for no reason is strong
as it is through to me now how

CHAPTER ONE
The Stage

"*WELCOME TO THE CITY OF LIGHTS, welcome!*" sang the recorded voice through the speakers somewhere above me.

A group of harlequin clowns with black and gold balloons tied around their ruffled, satin cuffs repeated the mantra as I walked past them through the streets, sticking to the shadows that I was born to.

If I were the kind of man that smiled, there'd be one on my face right now. Instead, I simply inhaled the scent of fried treats, spun sugar, and popcorn, soothed by the sounds of merriment around me.

Home.

The City of Lights was finally awake as

the night rose. People called it a magical place, a place where anything and everything under the moon could happen. A carnival that never moved on, a party that started, again and again, each night, one that everyone was invited to.

But there was a price. If you stayed too long, the magic of the city swallowed you whole, turning you into its victim like a prisoner on an acid trip. The surreal would become your reality, and the mundane the enemy, and you'd be nothing but a gaping maw of constant hunger, always craving that first high and never satisfied.

That was unless you were born and raised here. There weren't many of us, but there were enough to not be taken in by the City's lure. And it was a good thing, too, otherwise, there'd be no one manning the ship, and a big ship the City of Lights was.

Bars, cabarets, opera houses, restaurants, shows, events, and salons. The Corral, the Crystal Garden, the Ethereal Imperial Circus, The Rabbit Hole. The Carnivale. All the infamous attractions for the adult senses.

Every night, like a living thing, the electric

lights would display the full gamut of sin, luring and feeding the many visitors.

But it was the dark places that the lights cast shadows on that held me here and made me feel at home. The quiet corners, the shady alcoves. The breakrooms where the workers with sweaty brows took a beat or two to rest from their customers. The walk home on Esplanade Lane as the sun began to awaken in a marbled sky in a last hurrah to the end of a long night, where the last bit of the City's employees headed to their beds, always accompanied by a lonesome pair of lovers walking hand in hand, whispering and laughing softly to themselves in wine-colored voices.

It was my city, glamorous and grotesque is all its glory.

But tonight, something was different. Something inside me felt unsettled, as if something were waking up inside me, restless, wanting.

But the feeling was subtle enough that I barely registered it as I kept to the wall, my target in sight.

About ten yards ahead, the man crossed the

cobblestone lane. His hands were in his pockets, his dark long coat touching the ground, and every few paces, puffs of steam would bellow out from the grates below his boots as he meandered his way through the Night District.

Pepper Stone was his name. A high-stakes player Johnny-Come-Lately.

Pepper had been on Pop's radar for weeks now, ever since wiping the Wolf boys clean of ten grand. Whether or not he'd cheated wasn't the point. He was new. Flashy. Arrogant. And more importantly, he didn't stay to play.

When I rounded the corner, I checked to my left and right, preparing to cross. A troupe of jugglers and jesters passed by, their laughter singing in my ears. Up ahead, Pepper stood, body turned toward a hidden door in the wall.

I waited patiently as two dancers cartwheeled past me, one turning in my direction to wink. I crossed the lane, just as my target went inside.

I jogged the last few yards to the secret door that practically blended in with the stone façade. Hidden in the third knot of rock above a thin seam of door frame was the buzzer. I pressed the button and checked my pocket watch. I had thirty minutes before I needed to get back to the shop.

In seconds, a small partition slid open and a pair of dark eyes met mine.

"*Jasmine,*" I replied, my voice gruff from disuse. The partition shut once more and the door opened, admitting me in.

Mesmer was an old establishment, and its clientele came from all walks of life. Each night, the password changed. Secrets and forbidden desires held court. Big money and loose morals, small minds and hungry eyes.

I felt the stain of sin blanket me as I passed the threshold and entered the main salon.

Crooning music with a heavy, slow bass played from the stage. The club had a crowd of thirty or so people tonight. I scanned the smoky, dim room. Pepper was seated at the bar.

"What can I get you, sexy?" a lush feminine voice said on my left.

When I felt her touch on my bicep, I turned to look at her and shrugged her off with a shake. Her face was painted white, framed by cotton candy pink hair that really did look like spun sugar. She wore a blue sequined outfit that barely covered her goods, and her thin lips were stained raspberry.

I ignored her and made my way to the back. About ten or twelve customers sat at the long glossy bar, most facing the stage to the right. There were two stools unoccupied next to Pepper. I chose the closest one.

The bartender put a napkin in front of me. He had to have been over seven feet tall. Rail thin with muddy green eyes that narrowed on me in a flash of recognition. I knew what he saw; broad shoulders underneath a dark gray hooded-sweatshirt, hood-up, menacing energy. He didn't know me personally, but my instincts told me he knew *of* me.

He cleared his throat and tossed the frown, replacing it with resolve. "What can I get you, sir?"

"Water."

The man next to me, my target, overheard and laughed as the bartender walked away to get my order. "Water? Boy, you're missing out. Life's too short for temperance."

I didn't need to turn and face him. I could see him clearly in the mirror in front of me, but he wasn't glancing my way. Instead, he faced the stage

My water came, but I didn't touch it. I waited a bit. The music ended and started up a new tune, coinciding perfectly with the lights around us that changed to a cerulean blue. When Pepper's glass slowly touched down on my right, I reached back, straightening my leg so that I could get into my back pocket. I turned my head to the stage and froze.

She sat on a stool, her long legs crossed at the ankles, her knees open just enough for me to see a glimpse of ruffled panties. My eyes traveled back up. Breasts full, soft yet firm, bordering on spilling from a corset of powder blue. Her shoulders gleamed with an ivory shimmer, contrasting with the shadows of her collar bone and the delicate dip of her throat. A long, graceful neck, smooth and inviting, led straight up to a heart-shaped face of pure angelic beauty.

It was her eyes that trapped me, though. Luminous eyes that sparkled like frost and rain and winter skies, captured inside the white, feathery mask she wore. She was singing low, a sweet, sultry tune that wrapped around me, melting the ice around my heart. When she closed her glitter eyes and tossed back her head on a high note that pierced my soul, ribbons of blue silk touched the floor—her hair, soft, so long, so smooth.

Minutes, hours, years passed as I sat enthralled by her. Long after she'd left the stage, taking her blue lights and sultry jazz with her, my eyes stayed glued to the spot she once occupied, until the bartender's voice broke the spell.

"—sure you don't want anything else?" he was asking.

I turned and noticed immediately that my target was gone. Fuck. *Fuck!*

Grabbing my wallet, I threw down a ten and shook my head at the bartender.

"She's something, isn't she?" he asked, taking my napkin and wiping the bar down where my glass had been. When I didn't say anything, he must have assumed I didn't understand. "Blue. The last performer? She was just hired. Almost a week ago, actually. Such a voice. She's going to be a star one day, mark my words!" He grinned in a dreamy, stupid manner and walked away, pausing to talk to another customer.

Blue.

I felt a hand on my back and closed my eyes, feeling spiders and fire ants dancing under my skin. When I stood and turned, Cotton Candy was there again. She leaned in close and tugged on the string of my hoodie.

"Want some company tonight, big man? My shift's just ended. Come on, I'll make you feel so good." She licked her raspberry lips, her bloodshot eyes scanning my chest and shoulders.

I leaned forward and whispered in her ear, "Get the fuck away from me."

She flinched as if I'd slapped her and pulled her hand away. "Sorry…uh…"

I walked away, but not before glancing back at the stage.

Blue. Her name was Blue.

The house music was playing, my target was long gone, and the stage was empty.

What had just happened?

ONE CLICK ON AMAZON

Acknowledgments

I always feel that I never give justice to those that have been crucial to my stories, but I will do my best. Creating beautiful stories and books isn't a one-person job, and I am beyond grateful for those that played a role in the production of Skeleton King. Thank you all for believing in me, supporting me, and all your help in making this story the best it could be.

I'm going to start by thanking Murphy Wallace. Without you this story would likely never have been written, and I am so honored to be a part of this stunning collection. Thank you so much for including me in this incredible project.

My incredible editor, Kim BookJunkie. I

can't even with how amazing you are! I swear you are magic with how you make my words so stunning. I don't know how I got so lucky to have you, but I am. Thank you for all your meticulous work. You truly bring my books to a new level. More than an epic editor though, you've been a true friend.

My betas! Oh man, you ladies saved this book! It takes a special person to beta read. It's difficult to kindly criticize, especially with the gracefulness that ALL of you did. I was blown away by your willingness to be honest in order to make this story the best it could be.

Kathi Goldwyn. You've been with me since the beginning, and I cringe to think where I would be without your friendship and support. Thank you for always telling me what I need to hear, whether it's being a beta or just pure encouragement. You have been a strong pillar that I can trust, and I can't express how much help it's been.

Salina Anderson. Well, you saved my ass with this book. Your medical knowledge was detrimental to the realism of this story, and I owe you so much for that. Thank you SO much for sharing your knowledge with me. And on a personal note, thank you for being such an incredible friend. You have also been with me since the beginning, and your support for my art will never be forgotten.

Kween Corie. Girl, you have been such a cheerleader for me since I released my very first book, and I can't accurately express how your enthusiasm for my words makes me feel. Thank you for being an OG Babydoll and always having my back. Your feedback is always so helpful, but your friendship is what I'm most thankful for.

Wendy Rinebold. You were a first-time beta for me and you absolutely did not disappoint. Your feedback had a huge impact on the final version of this story, and I thank you for not only reading my words, but also giving me so much support.

Nikki Murray. Girl! I am so freaking glad I met you! While of course, your feedback on this story was extremely beneficial, I'm really just so thankful for our new friendship. I can't wait to see all the things you do!

Gizel Alvarez. My boo! I owe you so much

beyond just being an amazing beta reader. You have promoted and supported me since my very first book and have continued to be a huge support and confidant. Above all that, you have been an amazing friend. Thank you for standing by me.

Tania Renteria. Oh my gosh girl! Your support, love, and encouragement has been so important to me. I can't express how grateful I am for all you've done for me. Thank you so much for being an incredible friend and confidant.

Jay Aheer. This cover! Thank you so much for putting such a beautiful face to this story. I know I'm not the easiest to work with, but you gave me EXACTLY what I wanted. Thank you for your art.

Dani René. This formatting is GORGEOUS. I'm so proud to be a part of this project with you. Thank you for the beautiful job you did on this series.

Bloggers. Thank you so much for all you do for the indie community. The time you take to review, promote and talk about the books you love is extremely helpful to authors like me and means so much when you choose to post about one of my books. You really are so important to this industry.

Readers. None of this would be possible without you. There are SO MANY books out there to choose from, so when you choose to read one of my books, it really does mean the world. You talk about the books you love simply because you feel passionate about them and I think that's beautiful. Thank you from the bottom of my heart for reading and supporting my work.

Last but certainly not least, my Babydolls! You guys have no idea what you do for me on a daily basis. You're my solace, my safe place and I literally don't have words for telling you that you gave me a place to be me, and I owe so much to all of you for that.

ALSO BY

Series
Candy Coated Chaos (Sweet Treats #1)
Sweetened Suffering (Sweet Treats #2)
Cupcakes and Crooked Spoons (Sweet Treats #3)

Standalones
Anointed
R.I.P.

Anthologies
Thou Shall Not: A Dark Ten Commandments
Anthology
The Dirty Heroes Collection

ABOUT
the author

Charity B. lives in Wichita Kansas with her husband and ornery little boy. She released her debut series, the Sweet Treats Trilogy, in 2018 and is constantly working on her next release. She has always loved to read and write, but began her love affair with dark romance when she read C.J. Robert's The Dark Duet. She has a passion for the disturbing and sexy and wants nothing more than to give her readers the ultimate book hangover. In her spare time, when she's not chasing her son, she enjoys reading, the occasional T.V. show binge, and is deeply inspired by music.